A Madhouse, C
by Hamish Cra

ISBN 978-1-937520-49-6
Published by
First Edition Design Publishing
February 2012
www.firsteditiondesignpublishing.com

Cover Artwork – Hamish Crawford
Cover Design – Deborah E Gordon

Library of Congress Control Number
2012931726

Table of Contents

Acknowledgements

I know few people read this bit (and in an e-book, skipping is all the likelier), and I'm sure anyone who's passionately hated what they've read is looking for people to blame. But don't blame these people; they're all lovely.

For their great help and advice with these stories: Tom Gahan and all at First Edition Design Publishing, Alexandra Writers, Kirk Ramdath, and Alyson Fortowsky (whose *Laser* magazine was the original home of two stories here).

Frankie McQueen is a real band, consisting of Connor Muth, Scott Giffin, Scott Charles, Devan Forster, and Kelly O'Keefe, who asked me to write about their figurehead. I thank them for allowing me to reproduce it here, and encourage you to seek out their music.

I created 'Simba' with my brother Fergus for a Rundle College school play in 2003. The splendid performances of Alex Little, Ross Coleman, Morgan Ambrose, and Mike 'Hot Sauce' Bull contributed greatly to the characters whose adventures I've continued over the pages. The Drama teacher, Mr. Aaron Goettel, allowed me to write five plays over four years at the school, and he, Mr. Buchanan, Mrs. Kim, and Mr. Clark, all got me seriously thinking about writing and the arts.

The Charles Dickens Caper started as a final project for my Victorian Literature class at the University of Calgary. I am eternally grateful for my professor, Dr. Vivienne Rundle, who brought Dickens, Thomas Hardy, George Eliot et al so vividly to life that I was inspired to contribute more than the standard essay.

For reading over my stuff, talking about it, and offering general friendly support: Jeremy Wadzinski, Matt Stamp, Michelle Brooks, Teresa Lynch, Hasan Matar, Caroline Cooke, Erin Belden, Dan Smyth, Traci Martin, Elizabeth Gilliland, Leanne Wood, Zac Brewer, Tyler Curry, Tristan Lowe, Courtney Fidler, Rebekah Jarvis, Andrew Hopkinson, Mike Haws, and Sir John Wrightson.

And to anyone I left out, it was obviously because you were too significant to mention.

I owe enormous debts as a writer to Douglas Adams, Tim Burton, Robert Holmes, Ian Fleming, Dan Aykroyd & Harold Ramis, and Brian Clemens. Their work fired my childhood imagination, and they held my hand and guided me into the wonderful worlds of Oscar Wilde, Woody Allen, Arthur Conan Doyle, George Bernard Shaw, P.G. Wodehouse, Neil Gaiman, Lord Byron, F. Scott Fitzgerald, Larry David, and so many others. Also, my 'soundtrack' while writing this has been dominated by David Bowie, Kate Bush, and Wes Montgomery.

Finally, my wonderful parents (for being more supportive than logically dictates, and allowing me to answer the difficult questions in my own time), and above all, my brother Fergus and my dog Snowey. Like the great names above, my debt to Fergus can probably never be repaid; suffice to say, his youth belies the breadth of his wisdom, talent, and accomplishment. Snowey is the first sounding board for any idea, and so everything I've written has lived or died by talking to her (not myself; that would accomplish nothing!). Though I'm sure she would react with bemusement if she knew how much she has inspired me, I humbly dedicate these stories to her.

Thanks to the names mentioned above, and so many more whom I am privileged to call friends, the solitary burdens of writing have been considerably lighter. I hope you all know how dear you are to me, and your tolerance of my mild insanity has greatly enriched my writing and my life.

Simba and the Charles Dickens Caper

Chapter One

Simba and the Charles Dickens Caper

It was a curious quirk of fate: the very weekend that I, Simba, journeyed to the Charles Dickens Society retreat, the weather suddenly turned miserable. Work at the Institute of Learning-disabled Llamas [1] was often time-consuming and difficult—sometimes occupying almost three solid afternoons a week—and sometimes I wondered whether Udder Maintenance Technician was the right job for me. Yet the moment I got time to myself, I was wetter than Captain Haddock's duffel coat.

As the rain poured down on the car windscreen, and I cranked the windscreen wiper, I turned to my friend and colleague, Carroll, and reflected ruefully, "Manual windscreen wipers certainly are a chore."

Carroll glowered at me. "Let's face it, Simba, even excluding the headlights that flash in Morse code, and the speedometer that's now sitting in my lap, and the roof with a strategic hole over my head ... the last time this car was road-worthy was during the Second World War."

Carroll was a tried and trusted nag in these situations. In addition, her coolly beautiful features simmered with disapproval whenever I, Simba, landed in scrapes such as this. Nevertheless, I always trusted that my raw charisma and boyish good looks kept her interested.

"Say what you like about me, Carroll ... but anyone who insults my Citroen 2CV is a first-class ... meany! There, I said it, and I'm not sorry."

"Would you mind keeping your eyes on the road?" she exclaimed, as I narrowly avoided a pick-up truck careening the other way. "The last thing we need in this weather is a crash!"

"Sorry, Carroll, just trying to keep you interested." I flashed her my trademark grin; she responded with her trademark scowl. Ah, the rapport we shared was magic!

"So, Simba, answer me this."

"The answer's yes, Carroll, and I want two baby boys—"

"Let me finish. Why is a man of your, er, talents, a member of the Charles Dickens Society?"

"Well, I knew the curator of the society, Jasper Wilkins, from this whisky-tasting event ages back. I wowed him with my talk of adventure and intrigue, and barely a minute had passed before he asked if I would like to join. You wouldn't believe some of the luminaries who are members—let's just say I didn't bring my autograph book in vain!"

She chuckled. "It sounds to me that you're more interested in hob-nobbing than in Charles Dickens."

"Anyone who knows me knows that one of my greatest passions is Dickens, or the Bard as many call him."

"No, that's Shakespeare, actually. I bet you can't even name one book he's written."

I laughed. "Oh really Carroll, what kind of simpleton do you think I am? To seriously suggest that I would be such an impressionable idiot as to join a club I know nothing about, purely for a few signatures, the occasional wine-tasting, and preferred rates on certain hotels—"

"Name one. I would just like to hear the name of one Dickens book."

At this moment the imposing Victorian façade of Gad's Hill Place loomed above us. Framed in the eerie, damp night, it was quite a sight, and thankfully distracted Carroll while I considered her question.

"I'm so glad I brought you to this retreat, Carroll." She smiled warmly at me. "I'll need someone to help me carry these hatboxes." Her smile withered as we struggled with the luggage.

The footman stiffly bowed, took our luggage, and welcomed us in. We were directed into a well-appointed study, the rich mahogany and soft leather a welcome respite from the cold. Standing beside the fire was Jasper Wilkins.

Jasper was a tall, dapper, and genial forty-year old. He was clad in the requisite Dickensian gentleman's frock coat and wing-collared shirt, and it was possibly on account of these clothes that he greeted us with such a formal bow. However, a smile broadened across his cheeks and he clapped his arms on my shoulder.

"Ah, Simba, good to see you again!" he cried. "I'm so glad you made it to this Dickens retreat."

"Jasper, you old rogue, allow me to introduce my friend and colleague, Doctor Carroll Osborne."

"I am delighted to meet you, Doctor," Jasper purred, crossing over and kissing Carroll's hand. "Simba's mentioned you might come along, and I am glad to see he wasn't exaggerating about your great beauty and charm."

Carroll smiled. "Well, thank you. Please, call me Carroll."

"Yes, I was saying on the way up—" Sadly my anecdote about Jasper's inability to tell apricot jam from strawberry jam went unheard. Jasper was flirting quite outrageously with Carroll. And *she* was reciprocating his affections! I quivered with rage as I heard their banter. It was bad banter too!

"Tell me, Carroll, what do you do at the Institute of Learning-disabled Llamas?"

"Well, they offered me funding to continue my PhD. research project. There's some admin, a large amount of field work …"

I could listen to no more of this. I walked over to the far wall, and poured myself a large glass of brandy. I took a sip, coughed, and then poured a lot of soda.

"Something wrong, Simba old sport?"

"Wrong? *Wrong! WRONG!?*" I bellowed. "No, nothing at all, why do you ask?"

"Oh, Simba's just jealous," Carroll laughed. "He hates anyone looking at me the wrong way, it's almost as though we were married. Which we're not, I'm quite available by the way."

"Forgive me, Simba," Jasper said. "The last thing I would want to do is cause you any offence."

They both paused, and suddenly I felt quite ridiculous. Perhaps it was the fact that tears were streaming down my face. Carroll and Jasper gave me a hug and a cookie respectively, and I felt a bit better.

"I'll tell you what, to cheer you up, I'll give you a sneak peek at a little surprise I've cooked up for this weekend. It should put us ahead of the other literary societies for good."

"Is there a lot of rivalry between your societies?" Carroll asked.

"You'd better believe it," Jasper laughed. "The Thomas Hardy Society—malicious sods—have devoted a vast sum of money towards constructing a gigantic Hardy Holographic Mainframe, completely overshadowing the Dickens Digital Database we put up just two years ago. Well, don't worry, I think this time we've got them beaten."

He crossed over to a small ante-room, and we followed curiously. Inside the darkened chamber was a large metallic egg, humming away with the sound of greatly advanced technology. Or possibly a refrigerator.

"Allow me to reveal …" Jasper pressed a button, and a hatch hissed open. "Charles Dickens!"

Charles Dickens emerged from the capsule and stood before us. His hair was a long mass, and he had a neatly trimmed beard. He was rather short and looked very jolly.

"This is Charles Dickens?" I spluttered.

"Delighted to make your acquaintance, sir," he greeted. "I am the man himself. Or at least, as I've been told by your friend, a facsimile of him."

"A robot?" Carroll asked.

"An android, to use the technical jargon, but essentially yes," Jasper replied. "The team has slaved away for months. Using all the biographical and textual information, we painstakingly assembled a quantum matrix—in a way, re-created his consciousness. We've programmed him with every detail of Charles Dickens' life and personality, and as you can see he is an exact physical duplicate."

"That's ridiculous!" I declared.

"Just what I thought, young man," Dickens replied. "Yet here I am, with all my life-time memories intact, ready to begin anew."

"Not that, the bit about the exact physical duplicate. This is what Charles Dickens looked like?"

"It is," Dickens answered with a hint of hostility. "Do you pick a quarrel with my face, sir?"

"Well," I said, "You don't look much like Simon Callow to me [2]."

After a brief conversation with Dickens (at which he revealed he was getting quite into *Coronation Street*, much to my distress), he retired to his egg, and Carroll and I to our rooms. After an hour or two to properly coordinate my wardrobe for the next two days, I descended to greet the Dickensians. Only a handful of enthusiasts had arrived tonight, the remainder being presumably kept away by the terrible storm. Entering the

ballroom, we were instantly confronted with a gregarious, rotund woman with a greasy apron and a disinterested-looking young child.

"Good day sir, good day!" she called out to me. "And who might you be?"

"My name is Simba, madam, and this is Carroll. Whom do I have the honour of addressing?"

"I'll give you a hint. Here's my young nephew, he's a jolly chore, very wilful. I have a husband, who's rather child-like, so I'm the head of the household. This little chap here never realises the great sacrifices I've made, raising him by hand." She leaned towards me and winked. "Go on then. Who am I?"

"Er … I don't know, Pat Boone?" I returned her suggestive gaze with a boggle-eyed stare. I sincerely believed that I was being confronted with a madwoman here. I had never met her before in my life, yet here she was giving me arcane clues? What did it all mean?

"Oh Simba, it's Mrs. Joe Gargery," Carroll leapt in. "You know … a character, created by Dickens?"

"You don't look much like Simon Callow to me."

"Ah, yes, of course, you're 'in character'. Very droll, madam, very droll. Ah, Mrs. Joe, that would be from ... *Jane Eyre?*"

Carroll laughed. "Very amusing Simba. *Great Expectations*, actually; as if you didn't know that. Don't let him fool you though, Mrs. Joe, he's a real expert on Dickens. Try to put him to the test."

"Perhaps later," I blurted. "I'm in need of some wassail."

We walked off, Carroll smirking. "I knew it. You don't have a clue."

"Oh, I got one wrong. I knew you'd hold it against me. Now I'm going to have Dickens fans pestering me all night because you've said I'm an expert."

Behind me a tall man loomed. He had Gallic features, a large nose, and a tapered moustache. His nose came up and his moustache came down.

"An expert, eh?" he boomed. "Well, in which chapter does my character get introduced?"

"Chapter ... One?"

"Which book?"

"Book ... One?"

He glared at me, a cruel smile across his face. "Correct. You may have won this round, but remember—no one gets the better of Rigaud Blandois and gets away with it!" He strode off haughtily, his cape fluttering, a glass of wassail and a snack-sized sausage roll in his hand. Jasper appeared and beckoned us off to the side.

"Thank God you came, Jasper," I sighed. "This place is a madhouse, only with more elegant jackets!"

"Oh, don't mind the enthusiasts!" he said dismissively. "Old Doris and Chad can be a bit off-putting, but they're not bad really. They just enjoy getting into their characters."

"Chad? That man Blandois' real name is Chad?"

"Simba, you've got to get into the spirit of things," Carroll said, patting my knee. "I think it's rather fun, actually. I only wish I'd known we could dress up."

"Well, I should think there's a gown or two going spare that would fit you."

"Shall I leave you two alone?" I pouted. I moved to get up, but Jasper gripped my arm and stopped me.

"One other thing, Simba," he hissed, a cold fire in his eyes. "Don't tell anyone about Dickens, eh?" His face immediately brightened, as if he had never been troubled. "Just want to save the surprise. I knew you two would be able to keep a secret."

I agreed, and walked away with the express intention of getting into the spirit of the event. But after being stopped and interrogated by Scrooge, Edwin Drood, and a fellow called Dick Swiveller, I was in desperate need of some air, so I stepped out on to the terrace. The rain had subsided, and it was a cool, clear night. I looked up at the night sky and reflected on how seriously some take their chosen hobbies. I then congratulated myself on how exquisitely my new cream blazer went with my pith helmet.

"Simba!" a voice behind me rasped. I shrieked, and turned around, to be faced with the concerned face of Charles Dickens. "Come with me, there's an emergency."

I followed Dickens into his ante-room, through a secret passage. He showed me a letter that had been pinned to the trick door. This is what it said:

DEAR CHARLES DICKENS,

I KNOW JASPER DOESN'T WANT ME TO KNOW YOU EXIST[3]. YET I DO, AND I WILL NOT ONLY MAKE YOUR EXISTENCE PUBLIC, BUT I WILL WREAK HAVOC ON THE DICKENS SOCIETY. REVENGE WILL BE MINE!

SINCERELY,

JASPER WILKINS'S MORTAL ENEMY, WHO SHALL FOR THE MOMENT GO NAMELESS

Chapter Two

Simba and the Charles Dickens Caper

"Poppycock!" Jasper laughed. "This letter is obviously some kind of pointless practical joke. I can see no value in attempting to trace the writer."

It was a pleasant Saturday morning. The tempestuous weather of the previous night had given the new morning an air of serene beauty, in addition to great big puddles to go jumping in. As we sat in the private dining salon with a plateful of eggs, some bacon, and Special K, Jasper's indifference was met with hostility from Carroll.

"Jasper," she protested, "you've only to read it. It was clearly written by someone with extreme behavioural problems, who wants to get revenge on you. That doesn't worry you?"

"Let's examine the facts, shall we?" he calmly replied. "We have a threat to my Charles Dickens android. Even if the letter-writer knows of his existence—which is unlikely, unless a member of the Cybernetics Team blabbed about it—he has no way of doing Dickens any harm. The security protocols on that pod would take a genius of computer programming to get through, and even then, only I can activate or deactivate Dickens."

"It doesn't sound to me like Dickens was the one being threatened."

"Carroll, Jasper, enough!" I cried. "While I believe Jasper should be wary, I agree that the culprit has done nothing so far and may merely be winding him up. I suggest we stay close to Jasper. We'll be more than adequately equipped to battle any foe! After all, I've been involved in a few scrapes."

I was about to launch into a reminiscence on the three-headed Arabian camel thief, but sadly I was interrupted. I say sadly, but Carroll and Jasper both emitted what was seemingly a sigh of relief as the butler entered. Still, I reassured myself that such a reaction would be completely impossible, and it was probably just indigestion.

The butler announced that the first debate was commencing, and Jasper quickly finished his plate, drank his tea and departed. A few minutes later we joined him in a large stateroom. The numbers had swollen considerably since last night, and dozens of Dickens experts now milled about, in full character, eagerly awaiting the inauguration of this debate.

As I looked from one face to another, I realised that any one of these seemingly benign fans could have penned the threatening missive. My blood ran cold, and I took it upon myself to protect Jasper's life, no matter what the cost.

"Carroll," I whispered. "I hope you're looking out for suspicious behaviour. I want us both to be on our guard."

"Don't worry about me," she answered. "Just keep your eyes peeled, and try not to get distracted—"

"Ooh, look at that woman's dress. A tad unflattering I think." For some reason,

Carroll shook her head at me. Some people just can't detect a fashion *faux pas*, I thought.

The two teams stepped up to the raised stage, to rancorous applause. I noticed that some fans were really getting into the spirit, booing loudly at the team they opposed.

Jasper stepped up to a podium on the stage. He introduced the teams and announced the topic: which *Great Expectations* adaptation better captured the Dickens novel, the 1946 David Lean film or the miniseries with that bloke from *Fantastic Four*[4].

The debate was a lightning-fast exchange, each point matched and ruthlessly deconstructed. The acid wit and keen intelligence of the debaters both impressed and unnerved me. After all, could it be such a step from polished rhetoric and debating prowess to murderous megalomania? Probably, I supposed… but maybe not.

The debate took about three hours, with several breaks to watch pertinent clips from the films. I finally got to see who this

Mrs. Joe was, and found that she was less mad on the screen— albeit only marginally.

As the judges deliberated, one of the debaters suddenly got up and left the room. As he was feverishly adjusting his waistcoat at the time, I thought it best to follow him. He went down the hall, and into a small bathroom off to the side. He emerged with a newfound energy, as well as, I noticed, something secreted in his coat. He re-entered the stateroom, and I took a position in a small alcove above the debating platform. Concealing myself behind a handy curtain, I stood directly above the nefarious debater, prepared for any skulduggery.

Jasper (who gave me a momentary sideways glance, but luckily didn't blow my cover) rose to the podium to announce the judges' decision. As he prepared to make his announcement, I noticed a suspicious movement from the debater.

He was indeed secreting something beneath his coat, and as he adjusted it I could swear I saw a mat-black metal handle poking out. He regarded it for a minute and pressed a button on the handle. It looked very suspicious indeed. However, I could not move until the device was drawn. The sweat poured down my head, and fanning my face with my hat only did so much.

Finally, he pulled it out. Perched at the awkward angle I was, I still couldn't discern what kind of weapon it was. But the man pulled it out, had it under the table, and was pointing it dead ahead, at Jasper.

At some points in life, our destiny moves us ahead in ways that make our own individual decisions meaningless. So it was that I was pushed on to save Jasper's life, and so I grabbed the curtain to double as a makeshift parachute, and leapt to the stage.

My angle of descent brought me right on top of the evildoer, and I let out an ad-libbed banshee cry as I abseiled toward him. Despite his struggling, I got the better of him, and struck a blow to his head with my dependably sturdy hat. It was now that I realised the man was sixty years old if he was a day. Still, I thought, murder is a hobby for all ages.

I stood up, and cried out triumphantly, "Rest assured Jasper, the nefarious plotter has been caught, red—dare I say it— handed!"

I let out an ancient banshee cry as I abseiled toward him.

There was nothing but silence. I could not understand the horrified looks I was receiving. I felt a simmering hostility and resentment, as though if I stood there any longer, they would all leap on top of me. I turned to Jasper, and even he stood aghast.

"OK, so that wasn't the best punch-line, but even so…" I began.

"Simba, what the hell do you think you're doing?" Jasper yelled. "That was the senior chairman of this Dickens society, he's been a member for thirty-three years. Why did you assault him?"

"Some gratitude, Jasper. An old, weak chairman, and rather indifferent debater he may have seemed, but I will tell you what he definitely is … an attempted murderer!"

With that I pulled out the device, only to find myself looking at a camera. To rub salt in the wound of my humiliation, the camera flashed right in my eyes at that instant.

"Well, if it was just a camera, then why did the old fool have it concealed in his coat?" I protested. "I mean, what am I to think?"

"What kind of insane idiot are you?" called a voice from the audience. I recognised it as that increasingly annoying old harpy, Mrs. Joe. "Eddy always hides his trick camera so that he can take a candid photo when the debaters least expect it!"

"Ah. Well, you see … I didn't know that … and, if you knew the clue I received last night, well, you would understand …"

I trailed off, as the mob's anger was getting even more marked. With that, I ran out the back door and hid inside an empty wooden keg until I was sure that they had all passed. A knock on the keg reassured me that it was safe to come out.

It was Carroll. She smiled. "Well, at least you were paying attention," she sighed.

The rest of the day was fairly difficult, with everyone from the recovered chairman, Eddy (who, incidentally, was a big baby— all he ended up with was a black eye for Pete's sake!) to the tea-boys glowering at me. Despite the reverie of the day's activities, which distracted everyone to an extent, I still felt like a pariah, so I retreated to an empty room in the house.

The room was dark and almost deliberately dismal. The centrepiece was a large table, covered with cobwebs. As far as the eyes could see, decay pervaded. There was a wedding cake, now mouldy and disgusting, and many ornate plates and cutlery were laid out.

"The Hall of Great Expectations," a voice called behind me. I jumped and turned to face an exceedingly tall, wiry man of thirty, whose smile seemed rather sinister in the darkness. He had a pencil-thin moustache, which enhanced the eerie feel.

"Hey, Simba, don't take it too harshly. The Society can turn on people sometimes, but they forget these little trifles very easily."

I rolled my eyes, and chuckled. "Wonderful, but that still leaves me with the rest of the weekend to endure." I stared at him. I recognised him from the festivities last night, where he had been disguised as Edwin Drood. "Who are you then—or rather, what is your real name? I'm a bit fed up with the guessing games."

"Ah yes. Bert Basildon," he announced, with a slight bow. "I'm one of Jasper's 'inner council' so to speak. I helped him design that Charles Dickens android no one's supposed to know about."

I nodded. "I know about that one. I'm a friend of Jasper's too."

"He's a good man, Jasper, but rather quick to cut you loose. We had some disagreements about that android, and he dismissed me from the team because of it. Still, I'm not one to hold a grudge. I don't know about him though."

"Well, that rules you—" I started. I intended to end the sentence with 'out', but not knowing this chappy very well, I thought it wise to keep my cards close to my chest.

"Sorry?"

"That rules … that really rules. Congratulations." I started pacing around the room. Interesting though this Bert Basildon was, now that the conversation stopped, his continued staring at me, coupled with his skeletal frame, made him a slightly uncanny companion. Anything to relieve the silence at this moment would have been welcome, except for a mad Charles Dickens trying to kill us.

Well, guess what came through the door right then?

"Ah Charles my good man," I beamed, seeing him in the doorway. "Do come in, please." I stared over at him and found his eyes glowing. The effect reminded me of my aunt after she'd been, as my mother euphemistically put it, 'on the sauce'[5]. "Anything the matter, Charlie boy?"

"Must kill," he replied in a monotonous drone. "Must kill."

"Really? Must kill, eh? What could you possibly mean by that?"

Basildon nervously edged towards the window. "Well, Simba, judging by his crazed expression, unbalanced stance, and hands outstretched towards your neck, I think he might want to kill you."

Before long the cobwebs were aflame, and the
Hall of Great Expectations was an inferno.

Dickens roared, and a cacophony of explosions sounded from his chest. "Now look here," I said, trying to keep my voice as measured and even as possible. "What seems to be the matter?"

And with that, Dickens grappled me in his arms and strangled me. He threw me against the fireplace, so my jacket was now on fire. I threw it off hurriedly, hoping the flames might distract Dickens. He merely tossed it aside, and before long the cobwebs were aflame, and the Hall of Great Expectations was an inferno. I could barely see anything, and as I finally blacked out, I saw Dickens's outstretched arm.

"This really could be the end!" I croaked.

Chapter Three

Simba and the Charles Dickens Caper

I awoke to the sight of Carroll, leaning over me, the light behind her making her seem quite angelic. I felt re-energised, and leapt to my feet.

"I'm alive! I'm alive! I can't believe it!" I followed my exclamations with an impromptu jig, and an improvised ditty to the tune of "She'll be coming 'round the mountain". When my euphoria had died down (about twenty minutes later), I thought to ask Carroll to what miracle I owed my survival.

"We found you in here unconscious, with Dickens about to give you a fatal blow to the head. Luckily, Jasper was able to deactivate him in time."

"Simba, are you all right?" Jasper asked gently. "I don't know how it happened, but don't worry, we'll be doing a thorough scan of all his systems and subroutines."

"I should think so too!" I spluttered, hoping my indignation would be evident even as I coughed up charcoal. "I'll have you know that you've irreparably damaged my favourite smoking jacket. While I will concede that it's poetic justice for a smoking jacket to perish in a fire, it still is a lamentable loss."

"That's not the worst of it, Simba," Wilkins intoned, his voice a sepulchral whisper. "Wasn't Bert Basildon in this room with you when it happened?"

"Yes, and a very strange man he is too. Why?"

"We found this." Jasper produced a burnt and charred scrap of a boot. The remains of the spat hanging around it confirmed that it was Basildon's, as did the name-tag inscribed into the sole. "It's pretty obvious, isn't it? He's … dead!" Wilkins trembled, a tear rolling down his stoic cheek. Carroll gave him a reassuring hug.

"Hey! Who just survived a homicidal attack by a Charles Dickens android?" I barked.

"I already gave you a cuddle, Simba," she pointed out.

"It was pretty cursory."

Carroll sighed. "Could we get back to the topic at hand? Simba, what happened? Did you see Dickens's programming change?"

"No, he was like that when I first saw him."

"How could it have happened?" Wilkins asked plaintively. "Every subroutine has a thousand automatic fail-safes. The first programme laid into his positronic brain is that he must never harm a human being. The only way to disarm them would be with the deactivation key, and even then there's a twelve-digit code that you have to enter in seven seconds."

"Blimey," I nodded. "In short, harder to get into than the tea room at the Pentagon."

"Quite," Jasper nodded.

"But he simply *must* have been reprogrammed," Carroll insisted. Jasper was about to repeat his 'can't be reprogrammed' rhetoric, but Carroll held her hands up sharply. "Who would have the know-how to do such a thing?"

"I'll have to think about that. There were only a few other people who even knew about the Dickens android. Assuming it's possible—to entirely corrupt the conscious matrix we created—it would take a phenomenal computer genius!"

*****

With no easy answers, I adjourned to have a soothing bath and a hearty breakfast. In the middle of my second round of bacon and eggs, a policeman popped in to ask me a few questions. I reiterated the information I told Carroll, and the constable admitted to being baffled. I pitied the poor fellow, unable to comprehend the complexities of this mystery. Frankly, it needed a detective of my own calibre to solve it, and that is what I told Jasper.

Unfortunately, Jasper had problems of his own. I found him in the large state-room, being heckled by Mrs. Joe and Rigaud.

"Listen, Jasper," Rigaud shouted. "The constitution dictates that, in a state of emergency, when the members of the Inner Council are unanimous—"

"Which indeed we are," Mrs. Joe interjected, rather superfluously. But Mrs. Joe was always one to get her two pence worth.

"Then the curator may be overruled," Jasper finished gloomily. "Would it help if I asserted that I know nothing of these incidents?"

"There was a great deal that *we* did not know," Mrs. Joe spat. "We didn't know you had made an android duplicate of Charles Dickens—"

"As soon as my Cybernetics Team returns my calls, you'll have the whole story," Jasper began, but Mrs. Joe's chainsaw voice kept blaring over him.

"...And we *certainly* didn't know that it could be reprogrammed to carry out violence and murder."

"That hasn't been proved yet!" I shouted. "Now listen to me, Doris and Chad." They both cringed as I used their real named. I smirked. "You two may believe yourselves kings of the hill, but Jasper is the curator of your society. Think of the good he has done, the amazing efforts to put this society on the map. Did he do it for petty reasons such as personal glory, money, or to get back at his high school bully? No! He did it purely to further the venerable study of one of Britain's greatest authors. I am disgusted that you two arrogant, trumped-up popinjays could take such a great man, and attempt to blame everything on him, just because he made an android without telling you, and it burned down a room and attempted to kill two people."

"You don't think that behaviour is a tad reckless?" Rigaud sneered.

"Reckless? Chad, my dear fellow, let me tell you a story. I once flew a plane the wrong way down a Heathrow runway, landing mere inches away from another plane taking off. I then sliced the wings off with the traffic control tower, and then I evacuated the plane, chucked a bomb aboard, and blew it up. Do I even need to mention that I don't know how to fly, or that I performed this dubious stunt while I was dressed as a pantomime horse?

"Now on the face of it, that may have seemed fairly reckless. But it may interest you to know that I had very good reasons for doing all of those things. The plane, you see, was covered with a form of corrosive bacteria that would have killed every single person in Britain in seventy-two hours. Only immediate destruction of that plane could prevent it spreading. And I wore the pantomime horse costume so that I could risk my life putting the bomb right next to the core of the bacteria. And if you tell me I deserve to do time for that stunt, then I will tell you the same thing I told the Old Bailey judge. 'Phooey!'[6]

Really on a roll, I concluded, "Jasper Wilkins may well have perpetrated the acts I bore witness to. However, what evidence do you have against him? Nothing conclusive. My friend Carroll, a fully qualified first-class clever clogs, believes the Dickens android has been reprogrammed. We need to find out how, by whom, and most importantly… *why*! And I propose to you, Doris and Chad, that I, Simba, am precisely the man to solve this mystery."

The assembled enthusiasts burst into a round of applause, and I bowed, thankful that my charm had claimed another victory, and that people were prepared to put that unfortunate Eddy business behind them. Rigaud and Mrs. Joe, however, stared at me frostily. After some brief consultation, Mrs. Joe solemnly announced:

"Despite our fears for your sanity, we will allow you the opportunity to solve this mystery. However, we must also observe the constitutional rules of the Dickens society. Curator Jasper Wilkins will be court-martialled at 10:00 a.m. tomorrow. You have until then to find new evidence and save your friend." She flashed a bitter, humourless smile. "I personally wish you frustration and failure in your endeavours."

"In that case, madam, I wish you incurable gout and irritable bowel syndrome. Good day."

I bowed again and took my leave of them.

Retiring to my room, I jumped slightly to see Dickens staring at me.

"Don't worry, Simba," Carroll said, whirring her sonic screwdriver around his head, "I'm just scanning him to see what caused the problem. There's no technical fault, so we're definitely dealing with sabotage."

"Simba, my dear fellow, I am mortified at the attempt I made on your life. Allow me to apologise."

"Well I should think so too!" I grumbled. Dickens's face was filled with a melancholy comparable only to my father's when I told him I wasn't a big fan of the Bee Gees. I softened, and asked, "Do you have any idea what might have caused it?"

"Carroll has explained that my circuits may have been altered. That, alas, seems to be a disturbing possibility. I would almost have preferred it if I had deliberately attacked you."

I blanched. Carroll squeezed his hand in sympathy.

"Don't you see?" he implored. "Now I have learned that I am no more than a puppet, at the whim of whoever has enough control of me. In life I prided myself on my own capacity for self-will, to use my voice to help others. Now I am little more than an empty shell, echoing the words of a dead man, who can be employed as a puppet to assassinate others. What worth are any man's actions when, at the push of a button, he is a rag-doll for another's fancy?" He bowed his head.

"Don't worry, Charles." He looked up at me. "I'll find who did this to you, and it won't happen again."

Although heartened by my words, the sadness still glimmered in his eyes. Carroll opened up his chest circuitry to run some more scans. She looked up at me.

"Simba," she whispered, smiling, "count me in."

"Ha ha!" I pranced about the room. "I did it! I knew I could melt that icy exterior! You're not so tough after all!" I skipped down the corridor, imagining Carroll's glare searing a mark into the back of my neck. But as I jumped down the spiral staircase, I reflected on today. A smoking jacket had been lost and a man missing presumed dead, certainly, but on the plus side, I had survived death, staved off a trial for Jasper, given

I pranced about the room.

Dickens some hope, and softened up Carroll. By Jove, I was on fire—literally last night, figuratively today! I felt so infused with goodwill that I needed some fresh air to further affirm my euphoria. I headed outside to a glorious late April afternoon that made me want to leap into song. The fresh air hit me with all the invigorating blast of a gun of, er, fresh air (all right, scratch that one). But anyway, I wandered through the gardens of Gad's Hill, smelling the beautiful posy of the spring flowers, and reflecting on how brilliant things were at the moment.

Then I came upon a sight of complete horror.

A macabre crowd stood gathered around a small lake down the hillside. A few unsavoury-looking Dickens enthusiasts were operating a ducking stool, and tied to it like a worm on a hook, gasping for breath, was Jasper Wilkins.

Chapter Four

Simba and the Charles Dickens Caper

My course of action was obvious: I would sooner wear a soft-topped hat with two-tone shoes than see Jasper harmed as a result of crazed Dickensian antics. Immediately I faced a conundrum: what could I do to save my friend? Rely on my low cunning, or my physical strength? Or perhaps I could rely on my physical charms, and outrageously flirt with the society members to such a degree that they would completely forget about their torture.

Eventually, I decided to abandon all logical thought and charge down the hill screaming. This time I took a Mongolian war-cry as my basis, but it still came out as: "AAAAAAARGH!"

"Uh-oh," I self-consciously muttered. I had drawn attention to myself but didn't have a clue what to do next. Luckily, they had left the ducking stool in its upright position, and Jasper was hurriedly sucking in air. But I rapidly sensed their anger rising, and I wondered if they had a ducking stool with my name on it.

"Er… hello!" I announced. Damn, I was hoping to confuse them, and unless they were like my tenth grade mathematics teacher, that sentence was unlikely to do the trick. I ran through my options, and thought of an exciting new one: why not insult them? As no drawbacks immediately presented themselves, I went forward with it.

"Is that a frock coat, or did a silkworm vomit on you?" I cried.

There was a pause. Confusion: excellent!

A voice piped up from the back. "Excuse me. Whom exactly were you addressing?"

"You! And your ugly friend! And any scoundrel who thinks that immersing my dear friend Jasper in freezing cold water is a good idea!"

"Actually," Jasper replied, his breath returned, "the water isn't that bad."

"It's really the principle of the thing I have a problem with," I added.

"Hang on!" a second voice cried. "That's the guy who tried to kill Eddy!"

"And now he's insulting us? The infernal cheek of the fellow! Get him!" The mob turned towards me and ran. Really, the sight of a dozen grown men running towards you is a terrifying one. I could do nothing but stand there, paralysed with fear, and close my eyes while my upper lip wobbled uncontrollably.

Opening my eyes a crack, I noticed that they had all stopped. I turned around, and there stood Carroll. "Hey, I saw some Thomas Hardy fans spraying graffiti on the front of the house!"

"What did it say?" the same bloke asked. (Why is it that there's always one inquisitive member of an angry mob, I wondered.)

"Er—'Dickens lovers go home'?" Carroll ad-libbed. I cringed; surely that wouldn't convince them?

"Let's get the f—ers ⁷!" They ran off.

"That should keep them occupied," she said. "By the way, congratulations on not losing your cool."

"Thank you for your help," I replied, choosing to ignore the sarcasm in her voice and put it down, again, to indigestion. I suppose the rustic delights of Kentish cuisine could make anyone ill-tempered. We dashed over to the ducking stool and untied Jasper, who was rather morose and taciturn.

Following this, we hurried to my car, and drove with all speed down the A229. "I suppose we'll head to Rochester, maybe even to Chatham if necessary," I suggested. "Frankly, I'd shack up in a demilitarised zone rather than return to that dreadful house! Those ungrateful swine, attacking Jasper when it's not even his fault!"

Once I said this, a thought crossed my mind. I hesitantly turned to Jasper. "It isn't your fault, is it?"

Unwell though he was, Jasper still cracked a feeble grin. "No, I can't say that it was. Though it may as well have been. Simba, Carroll, don't get me wrong, I thank you for the risk you both took. But my misery is so pronounced that I almost wish you would bring me back to that ducking stool and permanently submerge me."

Carroll patted his shoulder reassuringly. "Oh Jasper, don't you see, that's exactly what the real culprit wants you to do? Obviously, whoever's behind this knew that this would result from his actions. He specifically wanted you to be targeted. We've got to find this person. But what clues do we have?"

"As many as Ben Mulroney has brain cells!" I retorted. A second passed, and I wasn't sure if they had gotten my point, so I added, "Zero! And the situation is getting ever more desperate. A man has been murdered, Dickens is having an existential dilemma, and Jasper here is being driven to terminal depression." I leaned out the window, and shouted out to the pleasant Kent countryside: "Why? Why would anyone do such a thing?!" It certainly got the family across the field staring at me, but it didn't answer the question.

Undeterred, Carroll began thinking aloud, an irritating habit that usually meant she was on to something. "That fellow, Bert Basildon—his death hasn't been proven, first of all. The whole thing seemed calculated to demonstrate how out of control Dickens was. And we have no evidence that he died in the fire, and there was nothing outside to suggest he fell out the window."

"Lemuel Gulliver!" I exclaimed. "You think Bert Basildon was the culprit? Take it from me. I talked to the man—he was no more devious than a sponge. Creepy, I'll give you that—but a fellow can have creepiness spilling out of his stovepipe hat without being a criminal. Although Tom Cruise may yet disprove that."

"Time to get out and stretch our legs a bit, I think," Jasper interjected. "Why don't you pull in here? We can have a better discussion in this quiet country pub." We had pulled up in a beautiful green, surrounded by Tudor-style houses that had been converted into all manner of establishments. Luckily the green commanded an excellent view across the River Medway, all the way up the precarious cliff that led to Gad's Hill Place. If anyone was coming, we would be ready. Secure in this knowledge, we went into the local watering hole, Vincent Vedder's Vivacious Vintners. After a brief conversation with Mister Vedder, a cheery fellow with a passion for lutes, we found a quiet table at which to discuss our theories, plan a strategy, and quaff some claret. Wary of potential Dickensians on the prowl, we kept a low profile, and I even consented to remove my pith helmet.

A few glasses later, and I was still thrashing out Carroll's idea. "So, you think Bert Basildon faked his own death, knowingly setting off a chain of events designed to incriminate Jasper?"

"Maybe not," she mused. "But I don't think he's dead, and finding him will be the first step towards finding the culprit. After all, Jasper, you told me he'd said he helped you design the android. So he'd certainly be able to do it. As to why—maybe someone out for revenge paid him off." She turned to Jasper. "What kind of person was Bert, anyway?"

"Oh, he was a decent enough fellow," Jasper chuckled. "I liked him a lot, but he was the sort of person who deliberately antagonises others. We hadn't spoken in a few months because I dismissed him from the team. It was just because of other members saying he kept ignoring them and insisted on doing everything his own way. He blamed me for it, but the whole project was precarious enough, and it was my duty as curator. He didn't see it that way—blamed it all on me, became very bitter. We never really got back into our old ways. But really, Bert wasn't a bad person."

"Wasn't he?" I asked.

"Well, no," he replied insistently.

"Jasper, please, it was a rhetorical statement, casting doubt on your earlier assessment. As for me, I have to say that your theory is a load of cobblers, Carroll. I know, too bad, you're wrong for once in your life."

"Well, who do you think it is, Simba?" she asked, rather haughtily.

"Chad and Doris! *Hell-ooo!*" I blurted out, my voice taking on an unintentional musical tenor. "They obviously want to overthrow Jasper. They could quite easily have found out about Dickens and claimed ignorance as a way to impeach him. Why, Doris even wished me failure in my investigations. It can't be a coincidence that they love humiliating me, the one man they know is capable of defeating their nefarious schemes!"

"But even if your theory was correct, they'd still need someone like Bert to reprogram Charles Dickens."

"Damn, that's true," I conceded. "Are we ruling out extra-dimensional entities here? Because they could reprogram Charles Dickens without breaking a sweat. And I should know, because I met some once—"

Sadly, as I was the, well, third to admit, there was no time to recount my encounter with the diabolical Graas and their plan to cause toasters around the world to attack humanity[8]. After a bit of thought, my plan was formed.

I suggested that I drive back to the house now and search for clues, and they lie low here and come back this evening. To that end I gave them two jet-packs I stowed in my car for just such an emergency. We decided that, to signal them, I would fire off one of the flare guns I kept in my car for emergencies. Carroll agreed to this plan, even though she pointed out that it was unlikely that I would find anything, and that I was putting my safety at great risk by returning to the angry mob that I had insulted only a couple of hours before, and that even getting there was unlikely as I'd probably had too much wine.

Actually, now that I think about it, I don't really think Carroll did agree. But I went ahead with it anyway, because at least me being up there would keep the angry mob occupied, and I was confident I could hold them at bay. On the way back, I reflected on how my driving was as accomplished as ever, as I navigated the narrow roadways along the side of the cliff. In fact, I often thought that a few drinks improved my driving, and I resolved to test this theory more after this escapade.

I snuck in through the back door, and found myself in the stateroom. It was in complete darkness, so I switched on the lights. Staring at me were the same dozen members of the mob. This time, though, they had a leader: none other than Blandois.

"Surprise!" he shouted.

"Why hello Chad," I greeted, trying to remain chipper despite this nasty surprise. "Oh, I got that little gag, by the way. It's like a surprise birthday party. However, unless I am much mistaken, it's not my birthday. And I'm certainly not surprised to see your ugly face here, any more than I was to read about it in *Adam Bede*."

"You are a fool!" he bellowed. "Now, are you going to tell us where Jasper is, or aren't you?"

"Hmmm … nah."

"I should point out to you that I've sent away all the rationally minded fans, and agents loyal to me are trawling the Kent countryside looking for your chums. It's only a matter of time before they are found."

"Oh, not where I've stashed them away." I smirked, and it's amazing how a simple smirk can so palpably irritate so many people.

"You leave me no alternative. I challenge you to a Dickens trivia duel. We shall be asked a set of four skill-testing questions. If I defeat you, you will be forced to reveal his whereabouts."

"OK, I'll bite. May the best—and by best, I mean, one with the less stupid haircut—win!"

The process was rigorously formal. Our names were fed into the Dickens Databank—a vast mechanical beast, hewn from mahogany and brass, full of punch-cards of trivia—and the questions were printed out on a sheet of foolscap in front of us. As it produced the questions, it hissed and clanked, and steam emanated from its valves. It was the very image of a Victorian, steampunk-y idea of a computer. I fully expected to see Tim Burton at the controls.

As for the contest, it was a gamble, and it dawned on me, slowly and dreadfully, that I had no idea what I was getting into. Furthermore, I was increasingly concerned about Carroll and Jasper. Still, I summoned a force of calm within myself. Perhaps it was some ethereal spirit that visits upon all those in need of a bit of Zen. Perhaps it was my neural transmitters furiously summoning up every scrap of information I had ever learned about Charles Dickens. If the latter, it would explain why it didn't take very long.

Reproduced on the chart below are the questions we received, and our answers:

Simba

Where and when was Charles Dickens born?
Er ... Grimsby? And ... ooh, 1811? (X)

What was the 1897 silent adaptation of Oliver Twist titled?
Er ... Oliver Twist? (X)

Who played Bob Cratchit in the 1992 movie, The Muppet
Christmas Carol?
Ah-ha! This one I do know. Kermit, of course! (√)

Which 1970s rock band took its name from a character in
David Copperfield?
Another easy one! Ye gods, this is really my day. Uriah Heep. (√)

Chad/ Blandois

Where and when was Charles Dickens born?
Portsmouth, 7 February 1812. (√)

What was the 1897 silent adaptation of Oliver Twist titled?
The Death of Nancy Sykes. (√)

Who played Bob Cratchit in the 1992 movie, The Muppet
Christmas Carol?
What? Muppets? What treachery is this? I don't know, pass. (X)

Which 1970s rock band took its name from a character in
David Copperfield?
Micawber? Murdstone? No, no! It's all slipping away. (X)

Despite my late recovery, we still only had a tie. Mrs. Joe
arose and announced the result.

"In the event of a tie," she sombrely proclaimed, "the
contestant with the better haircut wins. The Dickens Databank will
produce the result." After an eternity, a punch-card popped out of

the bottom. Mrs. Joe picked it up and read it. Her face fell, and she scrunched it up and threw it away, muttering various obscenities.

"Well, well, well, looks like I won!" I danced my victory jig as a celebration.

"No! This contest was a disgrace!" Blandois pulled out a revolver. "It's time to put you away for good."

"Ah! Kill me if you like, but first, please tell me—were you behind the plot to incriminate Jasper Wilkins?"

"Eh? That's ridiculous! Everyone knows Jasper did it himself!"

"Well that's what the culprit would say, isn't it?"

There was sage mumbling of agreement. I sighed with relief that even the Dickens fans that remained, devoid of reason and sanity though they were, still recognised good murder mystery etiquette.

"Well, allow me to satisfy your curiosity. No, I didn't, I knew nothing about the Charles Dickens android, and I still firmly believe Jasper orchestrated the whole scheme. Evil I may be, but a plan on that scale is beyond my comprehension."

"Ah. Well, thank you for your honesty." I couldn't help but add bitterly: "Bloody hell, you were so obvious too!"

"Yeah, well, I am Blandois, you know. I am expected to be a bit evil."

"I suppose so." Thankfully, this witty banter gave me just enough time to slip off my pith helmet and fling it at Blandois. It hit his gun exactly—now I could finally tell my university roommate that all his vases had not been broken in vain. I dashed out of the room, and Blandois' sycophants were hot on my heels.

I climbed the stairs to the roof, and pulled out two devices: first, my flare gun, with which I fired my warning shot to Carroll and Jasper, and second, my trusty piton gun. I know, gentle reader, it is difficult to imagine someone carrying a flare gun *and* a piton gun around with them, but you'd be surprised how often my scrapes—and even trips to the shops—involve firing flares and scaling the sides of buildings. Just as they closed in, I fired a piton and slid to safety. Climbing down to the ground floor, I spied Dickens in the window.

"Here, I'll stall them while you get away," he smiled.

"Thanks. By the way, thanks for … you know … fixing the Dickens Databank."

"I did no such thing. Why, you won?"

"Yeah."

"Oh." A gloomy expression darkened Dickens's features. "I'm sorry to say it, Simba, and please take no offence, but that is a most peculiar occurrence. Indeed, terrified as I am of spontaneous combustion, there are more inexplicable phenomena."

"Oh, all right then. Well, must dash. Ta-ta!" I ran off to my car, and before long I was back on the road, simmering with frustration. After all, the entire point of my trip was to find clues, and instead I'd lost my upper hand and had to run away. Good gravy, Professor Plum could have done a better job! I banged my head on the wheel, which accidentally deployed the airbag.

"Hang on a minute," I ruminated. "The Dickens Databank was programmed by someone … someone who wanted me to win … but who? Think Simba, think! *THINK!*" Amazingly enough, bellowing "think" at myself repeatedly really didn't help me think that much, but I was sure that I had something.

However, my contemplation was swiftly derailed by the sudden realisation that I was being followed. Careening behind me was a vehicle at once funereal and comical. It was a hansom cab, running without a horse. That's right—quite literally a horseless carriage! Driving this cab was a man, his face concealed with an opera cloak, yet who wielded a whip in one hand and a gun in the other. The former was slightly redundant, given the absence of horses, but the latter did have one immediate use that leapt into my mind. Actually, come to think of it, if this fellow had the right sort of twisted mind, the former could serve the same purpose. Ewww!

"Wait a minute—the cloak, the twisted mind… Cecil B. DeMille! It's Bert Basildon! Carroll was right! He is still alive!"

My three revelatory exclamations were muted by more immediate dangers. Bert and I were traversing, at hair-raising speeds, the narrow road alongside the cliff. A deviation of inches either way would result in doom, of either the watery or the crashy kind. My driving was good enough, but next to that carriage, my Citroen was handling like Canada Post with a valuable package.

Fortunately, I was able to distract him in other ways. The car had a few optional extras installed. Believe me, in my experience one needs as many gratuitous technological implements installed in a car as possible. Except On-Star, that's just a waste of money.

First of all, I decided to put a bit of distance between us. At the touch of a button, a rocket launcher extended from behind my car, and shot me down the road at double my speed. Readers of the back-seat driver variety might wonder why I thought it would be a good idea to increase my already dangerous speed. And I did ruefully wonder the same thing as I was heading off the edge of the cliff. In a moment of panic I fired a grappling hook, which pulled me around the corner just in time.

Next, for my own safety, I extended two mechanical skis for balance. Fairly stable now, I needed some way to disable the carriage without causing its occupant to topple over either. In turn I ruled out the rocket launcher, smoke screen and oil slick as possibly a bit too lethal—unfortunately *after* I'd deployed them, but the blighter managed to avoid them, so what the hell.

Finally it came to me—a handy little device the I.L.L.[9] quartermaster liked to call "the Tag". It was a rope that fired out and attached itself onto the vehicle, forcing them to adjust their speed unless they wanted to ram into the back of you. Firing it, I briefly wondered if my insurance covered unforeseen gadgetry-related mishaps[10].

The trick worked perfectly. The carriage pulled back, and, satisfied, I stopped the car and decided to face my pursuer. He sat stock-still atop the carriage, and when I pulled the cape away from his face, an especially smug glance greeted me.

Wearing it with such bad grace I wanted to punch him, was Bert Basildon.

"Why hello Simba," he beamed.

"Yeah, well, I guessed it was you, you know."

"Yes, I was wondering how many computers I was going to have to reprogram for you to get that. Still, I think you'd have to agree that this is check-mate."

The car had a few optional extras installed.

Hamish Crawford

Chapter Five

Simba and the Charles Dickens Caper

Outwitted, there was nothing I could do but go along with Basildon's demands: namely, that I drive him to Dickens' house, where he intended to implement the final phase of his plan. Even beyond the fact that the man had a gun pointed at me, the car ride was awkward. Every film I liked, he hated; every film he liked, I either hated or had never heard of.

Eventually, we reached Dickens' house. "No false moves," he announced, as he ushered me out of the car.

"What exactly is a false move? I've never understood that phrase. Would it be like if I pretended to go right, but I actually went left? I don't know why it would be such a problem. You've got the gun! I guess that's the purpose of the warning, but I feel—"

"Silence!" he bellowed, and gestured with his gun around the back of the house. I was rapidly running out of options, and had no idea what his plan was. Somehow I had to get him to reveal his plan to me.

"So … I think you can tell me your plan now. I'm sure you're dying to tell someone."

"You'll be dying, in a minute… in an all-too literal way." A cruel smile crossed his lips. I wouldn't have minded, but that pun was so bad, even Roger Moore couldn't have made it work. Just for that I demanded he reveal his plan to me. Again the miserable sod declined.

"All right, don't reveal it to me. I'm not really that interested." I paused. "Why, though? In the words of Burt Bacharach and Hal David, what's it all about, Alfie?"

"You want to know why? Jasper Wilkins, that's why. The man pretended to be my friend, but then … suddenly my ideas were too much. The Dickens android was supposed to be *my* crowning glory. Then those simpletons on his project team said I was losing my grip. Their paltry imaginations couldn't conceive my genius. I left, and the sycophantic creep tried to shrug it off. It was then I knew I had to have my revenge.

"Reprogramming Dickens was easy, especially as I'd designed the complicated security system and knew the surprisingly simple way to override it. But now comes the *piece de resistance*. I'm going to use my creation to murder Jasper's beloved colleagues. The man who's ruined my chance of success will have his own ambitions crushed, and will languish in jail wishing I had killed him."

"To be perfectly blunt, I don't really think it was Jasper who ruined your chance of success. You're too highly strung. You've got to learn to relax." My soothing words of encouragement hadn't really worked; Basildon was seething more than ever, twitching insanely at me, his mouth wobbling so violently I thought foam was going to start dripping from it. Nevertheless, I pressed on. "Have you ever tried Clark bars?"

"That's it! I've had it with your prattling! The time has come to silence you forever, much to the relief of intelligent civilisation." Despite my resentment, I remained silent. There's something about having a gun aimed at your head that causes you to lose the power of speech. The only similar sensation I had was when someone hid a Skittle in a bowl of M & Ms, and so I was expecting it to taste like chocolate and it tasted sweet. Yuck!

I realised my mind was wandering, and that I should make peace with all the two hundred deities I believed in, thanking them for blessing me with a life of adventure, but also adding that I was a bit put out that they were so hesitant to prevent me from, as the young people might say, biting it.

However, in a flash of action, Bert was suddenly on the ground, the gun knocked from his hand. Carroll had leapt down from a turret. She was a blur of movement, legs and arms akimbo, in a graceful melee that involved lots of throwing Basildon over her shoulder, twisting his arms, and kicking his backside. Every move he made, she anticipated, and even his dirty tricks she caught and blocked. She hog-tied him to the drainpipe.

"You took your time," I said.

"Well, we had to inform the police, and then the jet-packs practically conked out mid-flight."

"I guess they are a bit clapped out. Oops. I wonder if they're still under warranty? Anyway, where's Jasper?"

"He's trying to find Dickens. Apparently, with Jasper absent from the post of curator for over four hours, our old friends Chad and Doris will ceremonially step into the breach. It's exactly the moment that any vengeance-crazed sociopath would want to release a berserk android. But he needs an activation key—"

"This key, you mean," Basildon responded. "I find it always helps to have a copy of important keys lying around, just in case you get fired from a project and want to wreak some vengeance."

"Do you mind not interrupting? We're in the middle of something here." I paused, realising the situation. "Oh." Basildon had wriggled off the drainpipe, even though he was still struggling to undo Carroll's knots. Lying on the ground, his feet in the air, he looked somewhat pathetic, but still managed a sneer as he waved the key around his neck with his foot. There was something highly eerie about his flexible, twig-like frame.

"The tables may have turned, but I can still get my revenge!" He pulled a cord with his teeth, and his cape inflated with a pneumatic wheeze. Using the cocoon, Basildon rolled away at a surprising speed.

"Quick—follow that cocoon!" I barked. Carroll and I pursued him, but the house was a large one, and Basildon's completely improbable head-start had us both bewildered and unprepared.

We climbed inside the nearest window, and headed to the stateroom. Although I could barely breathe from the full minute and a half I had been running, I still couldn't help but reflect on the bizarre events that room had played host to over the last couple of days. It is often said that we only measure weirdness by the standards of our own lives, which may seem comparatively strange or dull to another person. But frankly, *any* revenge plot involving android duplicates of Charles Dickens, scheming fans, an attack on an elderly man by parachute, and a cloak that turns into an egg, would hardly be considered normal, even by someone as naive of such terms as myself.

After the heat of the sun, the comparative coolness of the hall refreshed me. I was also able to retrieve my pith helmet; wearing that, I felt truly ready to face any foe. The stage was set, but where were our opponents?

Using the cocoon, Basildon rolled away at a surprising speed.

"Quick, let's head behind the stage," Carroll whispered "Basildon might have a head start on us, but he can't have gotten that far." Proving her point, we were seized by two heavy-set men and pulled into a tight and dank alcove. The ace up my sleeve—

my element of surprise—had slipped out into a puddle.

"The police will be on their way soon, Basildon!" Carroll hissed. "You're finished!"

"That may very well be true. But they'll be too late. You see, I believe it's now time for the curtain to rise!" Basildon camply checked his pocket watch to confirm his self-satisfied announcement. On cue, the curtain went up and Mrs. Joe strode towards the podium. Her insufferable pomposity was even more acute when I realised that she was going to die and Jasper would get the blame. From the opposite end, Dickens strode towards her.

I desperately hit my time-honoured panic button: I stomped on my captor's foot and legged it to the stage. Carroll quickly conked the pair of them out with her combat prowess. And so, while Mrs. Joe took her place, the audience's attention was divided between Dickens and me crossing from opposite sides. I ran toward the podium and tried to push Mrs. Joe away.

"Listen to me, get off the stage! You're in great danger!" I blurted.

"What ever are you talking about?" she sniffed. She then saw Dickens striding forward, and recoiled in horror. "What is this? Are you responsible for this?"

"No, but listen—" I tried to explain, but I was rather panicky and short of breath, so the result sounded fairly incoherent. Mrs. Joe ran around the stage, seemingly trying to decide whether she was more horrified of Dickens or me.

"Someone help! This ruffian is using Charles Dickens to murder me!" she squealed.

"Listen, you silly woman," I spat, "Thanks to your stupid habit of jumping to conclusions, that's exactly what everyone will think. But I have nothing to do with this…" She suddenly froze, and stared in shock behind me. I turned, to see Dickens straighten his posture. The crazed glow in his eyes dimmed, and he removed the control key from his coat, tossing it to the floor.

"I have done it!" he exclaimed. "Simba, I overrode my controls. I reset them myself. I am a puppet no more." He walked over to Mrs. Joe. "Madam, allow me to introduce myself. Charles Dickens, at your service." He proffered his hand, which she received tentatively. "I must say that your treatment of Jasper

Wilkins is appalling, and I demand, on his behalf, a formal apology and substantial compensation."

Mrs. Joe instantly regained her frosty composure, and Blandois joined her on the stage to form their familiar two-faced sneer. He said, "I am sorry to say that the Dickens Society has certain rules, and we had to enforce them for the good of the members."

"Listen to me, you old trouts!" I shouted, bearing down on them with burning rage. Sadly, my tirade was interrupted by Basildon running onto the stage, wringing his hands in despair.

"No! No! You were supposed to complete my revenge. Jasper, I had to get revenge against Jasper!" Carroll and Jasper walked on-stage. Carroll gestured out to the audience, and two police constables quickly stepped onto the stage, grabbing Basildon. "What about my revenge, you useless slab of circuitry?"

"Nonsense!" I roared. "Dickens has proven himself to be capable of free will. He's more human than you'll ever be, you vengeful parasite!"

Basildon lunged towards me, but I held him back with a knock on the head by my pith helmet. The officers dragged him away, and the revenge on Jasper Wilkins was foiled.

"So Basildon was still alive," Mrs. Joe said.

"Yes, of course he was!" I barked. "Do try to keep up!"

"Well," Blandois said, moving toward Jasper, "I supposed we must apologise for our behaviour. Sorry."

"Sorry," added Mrs. Joe. I was aghast that those two could think that this would make up for the indignities they had foisted on poor Jasper. He seemed completely unfazed, almost shell-shocked by the whole incident.

Then, a group of people took to the stage. The leader, a stocky fellow, stepped forward, waggling his finger at Mrs. Joe and Blandois. "Oi, you two! Remember us? We, and a few hundred like us, are the Dickens fans you kicked out when you tried to take over the society. Well, guess what? We're not bloody 'appy. In fact, we're instigatin' proceedings to oust you two from the club. We'll see that Mister Wilkins receives full compensation." His speech was received with mumbles of assent from the group. "Oh, and from now on, we're bloody well calling you Chad and Doris, you hear? Sling your bleedin' hooks, you beggars!"

And finally, in a moment that caused me to fill with warmth and hope, Chad and Doris were led away, complaining and shouting at each other. Ahhh, even writing about it fills me with inspiration. I considered that I certainly owed those two hundred deities a few candles at Christmas, because things worked out quite perfectly.

With the mystery finally solved, Jasper, Dickens, Carroll and I headed out for a celebratory bottle of Dom Perignon at Vincent Vedder's Vivacious Vintners. After Jasper had revealed that he was going to have a holiday, Carroll asked Dickens about the future.

"I am glad you asked," he replied, grinning. "Jasper and I will take the next aeroplane out of Britain. We are going to commence an excursion around the globe. Since I have this additional time, I will use it to broaden my horizons, and enhance my understanding."

"And, er, Carroll?" Jasper asked. "When I get back, might I… er, give you a call some time?"

"Of course!" Carroll laughed, hugging him. They even shared a kiss, which was a bit too passionate. I cleared my throat pointedly before it got into 'high school make-out' territory.

"Let's focus on the present—I think a trip is an excellent idea! I've written a few books on travel if you need any ideas. I'd recommend *From Core to Stratosphere*—although take my advice and avoid the core, it's ridiculously hot this time of year. And, actually, pretty much any time of year."

"You should get it, Charles," Carroll added. "It's very funny."

"Yes … I shall," Dickens replied hesitantly.

"I'm sure you're surprised to hear that you aren't the only one with literary prowess." Dickens had to turn away, and I could swear for a moment that he was shaking with laughter. But, knowing that was impossible, I concluded that androids, too, must suffer from indigestion.

Jasper sighed. "I definitely need a break from the Society. All this organising and worrying, it's made me lose sight of why I joined—to enjoy Charles Dickens' writing more. I think I need a break from all this fuss."

We drank a toast to Dickens, and another to seeing the back of Chad and Doris. Just as we were having a really good natter, two men strode into the bar and stopped at our table. Jasper glowered.

"Hello Jasper," he trilled. "Hello all, Bobby Billbat, Thomas Hardy Appreciation Society. Heard you'd made a Charles Dickens android, and I wanted you to know … two can play at that game! I hired the same Cybernetics team and everything[11]!"

Standing next to him was an exact duplicate of Thomas Hardy, looking embarrassed.

"I can't believe this!" Jasper yelled, as they walked away.

"I wouldn't worry," Carroll said calmly. "His circuitry's sticking out."

"*That* was Thomas Hardy?" I spluttered. "He doesn't look a bit like Albert Finney[12]."

Epilogue

Two months later, I was relaxing in my Westminster abode, ready to go out to dinner with Carroll, when I was flicking through my mail. In amongst the usual fliers and death threats, there was a postcard from Australia, signed by Charles Dickens and Jasper Wilkins. I showed it to Carroll, and we recalled our hair-raising adventure at the Dickens Society retreat. I hasten to add that I resigned from the Society not long after that incident—the ill will felt because of Eddy's bash on the head was surprisingly widespread.

Anyway, the card read:

Dear Simba & Carroll,
Having a lovely time. Weather fine, wish you were here.
Best wishes,
Charles & Jasper.

"That's the best they could come up with?"

"Well, remember," Carroll replied. "When Dickens was alive, it was probably still an original postcard greeting."

As we headed to the door, Carroll paused. "You haven't— forgotten anything, have you?"

"Nope," I answered. "I'm absolutely positive."

"You don't remember what day it is today?" she asked, her voice becoming slightly more threatening.

"Well, it's the sixteenth, I suppose. Why do you ask—late paying some bills?"

"So you can't remember anything particular about today? Anything special?"

"Nope. Nothing at all special about today as I recall. And if I say so myself I'm pretty good at remembering important dates, so if I've forgotten it, it can't be even remotely important."

"Ah," she replied curtly.

That didn't bode well.

Coming next month:
The One Where Simba Forgets Carroll's Birthday

Fin.

Hamish Crawford

Awake

12:27 a.m. One glance at the alarm clock and the calculations begin. I have to be at work for 8:00—factor in eating my cereal, getting my shower, and the rest of the morning routine, plus the drive in, should put my wake-up time at 6:00. I lean over and check the alarm, which is set to 6:15. Of course, I probably subconsciously set it late so I'd have to miss breakfast. No matter how bland it is, I always regret it and my first step at the office is usually the washroom.

But wait. Today is … was Friday. I sigh in relief, lean over and turn off the alarm and bask in not having anything to get up for in the morning.

Sleep has always been a commodity, something I've struggled for, and I've often wondered if it's worth it. Of course, everyone has nights of staring at the clock and cursing that coffee they had after five. But for those people it isn't a regular occurrence, and they can take steps to prevent it. For me, every night is more or less a restless one. Even sleeping pills don't help. Unfortunately I'm scared to take more than two a night because I've always been scared of pills and Heath Ledger has confirmed my fears.

I remember being a kid, how sad I'd be after those bad nights' sleeps. Saturday was the worst, because I was wasting my socially sanctioned lie-in, and the Monday morning early start was an escape velocity I could hardly contemplate. When I shared a room with my brother, the efflatus of his snores droned a smug reminder of his comfort. Whenever I looked over at him I would see unvarnished serenity, and curse it. My own face, so I'm told, assumes a frown whenever I'm lucky enough to be observed unconscious.

The irregular sleeping habits stayed with me. My friends asked me why I didn't just take a nap in the afternoon, as they often did if they were planning a night out. But naps destroyed the fragile equilibrium of my conscious hours. I'd wake up to find I'd overslept, I felt a wreck, and I was afflicted with that freak mutation of morning breath that lingers all night, no matter how much mouthwash and brandy I gargled.

It was slightly better when Martha was here. At first I was highly uncomfortable having someone sharing my bed. Our first chat about it was pretty ridiculous, especially when I thought about the solitude. She didn't even think about it; she just laughed and said I would get used to it. And after a solid week awake, I did. In fact, for about three months I slept more soundly than I can ever recall sleeping in my life. Still not well by a normal person's standards—I kept count, and my best was six hours with no wake-ups—but somehow having someone else close, after the physical rebellion, weakened my mind's barriers.

When Martha moved out it was only on a trial basis. I could hardly dispute her reasoning; things had become a little too close for comfort, and we both needed some time apart. Or at least, that's what she told me. The several weeks (OK, I kept count of that too: three weeks and two days) have seen some of my poorest scores—maximum: five hours with four wake-ups, mean: just under four hours. Oddly enough, the detailed recording of my sleeping habits soothes me in the way a good night's sleep probably would.

At 1:47 I decide to switch the light back on and record my totals for tonight. I think I'd fallen asleep somewhere since 12:27, when I definitely checked the clock (sometimes I have dreams about checking the clock, and it being four in the afternoon; my subconscious can't fool me). I decide to record 80 minutes with one wake-up, even though it remained moot whether I'd been unconscious at all.

My lengthy insomnia experience has allowed me to appreciate and classify different modes of sleep. After a time, like an engine over-revving without petrol, the body will physically render itself unconscious. The mind however remains active so there's this black-out period where one is acutely aware of being unconscious. It's as close as I ever hope to come to being buried in quicksand; a kind of mental suffocation followed by a wrenching heave back into being wide awake.

Keeping score and taking notes seems a uniquely male way of coping with life's hardships. It's the same instinct that encourages inmates to scrape each day endured into their prison cell wall, as though a wall covered in ticks is some kind of monument to their suffering. Numbers follow us everywhere, and none more acutely than the time. As a result of being constantly tired, I'm constantly behind, and late for most things. Punctuality is a luxury of being well-rested, able to spring into action with consummate ease and bemoan the shabby, shuffling zombies for their tardiness.

Thinking of things to think about takes up some time. Lists are an easy one: ideally boring enough that one drops off in the middle of them. However, 'ideally' remains an important qualifier. I've made lengthy lists of Herculean boredom: books I hope to read, restaurants where I should have left a bigger tip, James Bond villains ranked best to worst (Goldfinger and Hugo Drax are an obvious top and tail, but where to fit, say, Kamal Khan?). Each list is embarked on in the hope that sleep will postpone its conclusion: when that conclusion comes, and the eyes still dart around the room, all that can be done is to hope their usefulness is redoubled when I switch on the light to write them all down. This has proved effective. One morning I awoke with pages full of anagrams of my co-workers' names. Seeing haphazard letters cluttering a page in daylight was a refreshing change from the nocturnal glow of blood-red digits.

These comforting statistical exercises are also a bid to keep my mind distracted from its natural preoccupation: the full-on depressive 'long night of the soul'. As a child this would often be confined to mere bump-in-the-night fears: the distant mechanisms of the fridge and dishwashers always sounded like different kinds of supernatural intrusion. One of my most clearly remembered dreams of youth is simply me, sitting in the living room of our old house, glimpsing a silhouette of a man holding a knife. The black outline, the poised blade, and the mundane setting left me terrified for weeks, and the boundaries between awake and asleep were for the first time suspended.

Though these fears still manifest occasionally—a disembodied crash that sounds like a burglar but is inevitably the destruction of a poorly balanced plate—they seem unaccountably juvenile in comparison to the long night of the soul. My first one was on a family trip with my aunt, when I was about eight. It was shortly before my aunt went back to Britain. I pondered the fun of her stay, considered the distance of her home, and the uncertainty of her returning. The thought of my young cousins growing up and my own summer and, by extension, youth slipping through my fingers filled me with a deep chasm of unvarnished despair. I sobbed silently for what seemed like hours.

Subsequently, this despair has taken many forms: it's encompassed my parents, my dog, my brothers, the friends I'm close to and distant from, and now Martha. Somehow, with no one else around and nothing else on my mind, the lack of intimacy in the world unravelled before me. There was no way I would ever be able to sit someone down and tell them I love them without prefacing it or putting tongue into cheek. This paralysing remoteness has always gnawed away at my soul. I always conclude such musings by promising myself that I'll do something different tomorrow, savour the moments, and say those words. But the jollity of morning mutes those intentions: the glow of sunlight somehow calcifies those sentiments.

I never told Martha I loved her. She may never come back, and even if she does it may not happen. Or at least, not the way I want it to; not the way I say it now, to myself, over and over again. And now, with the night yawning ahead, I have all the time in the world with nothing to do but regret it.

Frankie McQueen:

A Potted Biography

Frankie McQueen, in an era blighted by committee-written synth-pop, drug-addled celebrities, and Joaquim Phoenix with a hobo-beard, represents a welcome ethos of integrity, of old-fashioned graft, and sounds so intense they leave shredded cerebella like blown roses in their wake. It is hard to believe how this legendary rocker has stayed out of the limelight, to the extent that many believe him to be as fictitious as Chris Gaines and the Eagles' Farewell Tour. But real he is, and for him the road to stardom has proved rockier, steeper, and more covered with unexpected pointy bits, than most.

Born Franklin Delano McQueen in Glasgow, to respectable haberdashers Jock and Fiona, the rock icon of the 21st century could not have started less auspiciously. While his future seemed to lie in making hats with his doting parents, Frankie knew that early-80s Scotland needed a new sound to go with the vibrancy of deep-fried Mars bars, the Edinburgh Fringe Festival, and feeble gags about kilts. After being expelled from three schools because he didn't take part in knife fights, he landed a gig as studio engineer for seminal post-punk/jazz fusion band The Baked Bean. McQueen had no sound mixing experience, but for The Baked Bean, any recording session that ended with a full complement of drum kits and teeth was a result. For the next year McQueen guided the Baked Bean through notable successes such as "Funky F***er", "You Say Funk, I Say F***", and "What's the Name of the Next F***ing Song?". But McQueen knew when to move on: the Baked Bean's popularity was waning (partly because no one could tell their songs apart), and more tragically, his hard living took its toll. Legend has it that McQueen can be heard vomiting into the lead guitar towards the end of "F*** Funk".

Whereas vomiting in the workplace is frowned upon nowadays, in the mid-'80s it was a lucky break (how else can we explain the success of Air Supply?). Record executive Julius Gerrard, thrilled by the audacity of the stunt, offered McQueen a contract. He moved to Canada and toured for three months before he picked up a guitar. McQueen's learning technique was typically idiosyncratic: he is the only musician to have learned his instrument by osmosis, in this case standing very close to Neil Young over a period of two months. But it worked, and before long, Frankie had broken records across the country. Unfortunately, he did this by smashing vinyls and CDs over his head, which was largely believed to have hindered sales.

With this misunderstanding out of the way, McQueen achieved new heights of popularity. A touching moment opened his return to Glasgow in 2003: Jock and Fiona appeared on-stage and presented him with a fez, a reconciliation that brought Frankie to tears, and brought many fans to tears when he went to get a coffee with his parents instead of playing the show.

A serial husband (he currently lives with his fifth wife, 71-year-old Canasta player Dame Flora McQueen) and cereal eater, McQueen's 'salad days' are behind him: gone is the impetuous rabble-rouser who lit his trousers on fire while snorting a line of ants (his posterior is tender to this day). The accolades keep coming, though: *NME* raved, "Frankie McQueen makes me wish a write-up in *NME* meant something anymore," while *Rolling Stone* ranked him 15th on "We Just Make Up These Lists to Piss People Off, You Know". And McQueen has taken advantage of emerging technology: while he thought iTunes was a Tommy Tune-starring follow-up to *I, Claudius* and MySpace was his apartment, he is a prominent presence on both (much to the relief of execs worried about more 'record-breaking'). And there is a touch of Lady Gaga in McQueen's endearing weirdness: in his case, he believes his song-writing genius will escape through his nipples, and so has worn a sports bra on-stage for many years now (it also helps combat the inevitable upper-body sagging most aging rock stars are prone to). But there can be fewer more gracious music stars: Frankie will stop and chat to any fan passing him in the street, including some who have never heard of him. On-stage, he continues to make magic (and selflessly blame any mishaps on his backing musicians), and, barring ill-advised experimentation with the lute, we can only hope he will continue producing hits for many decades to come.

The Anarchist Penny.

The Anarchist Penny

A hobo once said to a banker,
He didn't quite know how to thank her.
For cutting his phone,
And foreclosing his home,
He employed a terse *lingua franca*.

Some called it a mistake, others called it an anarchist ploy to undermine Canada's Centenary. It was a serious enough matter for Lester B. Pearson, already in trouble with a minority government, to dismiss a high-ranking cabinet minister under mysterious circumstances. Despite Master of the Mint Norval Alexander Parker launching an inquiry, the whole incident was quietly hushed up and handed over to conspiracy theorists. The offending coin was never formally acknowledged. After all, at the end of the day, no one could offer a more plausible explanation than a perforation error at the Royal Canadian Mint. Whoever was really responsible probably retired in obscurity, never knowing the legacy of his mechanical corner-cutting.

In 1967, a Centenary penny was issued with a limited edition rock dove reverse. A handful—probably less than twenty—suffered a grotesque mechanical error. The steel plate upon which the coins were struck was badly aligned, and the punch press savagely hit the obverse. As a result there was a messy hole drilled directly into the Queen's temple, and the rogue stylus compounded this felony by stamping a moustache-like squiggle above her mouth. It was a disturbing image, and though neither the Queen nor most Canadians ever got to hear of the affair, it became an urban legend of Chase Vault proportions amongst numismatists. Simply because of its notoriety—and because all existing examples were believed to have been located and destroyed by the Mint—an intact "Anarchist penny" would be worth around $500,000.

(From Xavier Lucan, *Penny-Pinching: An A-Z of Numismatic Howlers* (Coin Lovers Alliance Press, 2007).)

Of course, Audrey thought, I'd have to get the lunch rush. It was the usual riff-raff, and Audrey, whose banking information was chronologically arranged and colour-coded, couldn't believe people could be so lax in managing their accounts. Blank forms, accompanied by cries of "How the hell was I supposed to know that?" elicited no sympathy from her. A bit of reading would clear up most people's confusion, but apparently the bank wasn't important enough. A particularly odious man, wearing loathsome sandals even though it was a chill October day, sauntered in with 969 pennies. When Audrey insisted that she could not accept them, he became crazed and his already-bulging Hawaiian shirt practically decompressed.

"Won't accept them? Pray tell, madam, why? Are pennies not legal tender?"

"Yes, sir. But they have to be rolled up—bank policy."

"Ma'am, would you care to explain to me the actual *point* of pennies? I never have enough of the little bastards to make up exact change, but my wallet, to paraphrase the Bard, still runneth over. Do they breed? Are they invading? I think we should be told!"

"Sir, it's bank policy. In fact, looking at your account balance, you should be very grateful for pennies. You have twenty-three dollars and forty-seven cents. That's gained sixteen cents over the last eighteen months simply from being in our Premium Savings Account."

For some reason, this did nothing to assuage R.J. Simkins of Boko's Holiday Home Apartment B. With a cry of "This isn't money. It's just ballast!" he released the tidal wave of pennies onto Audrey's desk. She decided to leave it to Grolsch to sort out when he came on. He had it coming: he always adjusted the seat-tilt, adding ten minutes of knob-cranking and unexplained pneumatics to every shift.

However, one penny caught her eye. While ostensibly the same as its 968 comrades, it was misshapen and had a slightly more coppery tint, which numismatists would attribute to rust. Audrey silently gagged, grabbed the coin and stuffed it in her pocket. She quickly walked outside, checking around her that Mr Griffin's bulbous eyes weren't anywhere nearby.

Audrey bypassed her usual lunch destination, 'Ole!', for the slightly farther and more expensive 'Joe's Cup of Joe'. She ordered a chicken teriyaki sub and black coffee, paid $7.18 with exact change, and sat in the corner booth to reflect on the implications of her find.

For a brief second she was paralysed with fear, thinking she had thoughtlessly given the coin away, with her automated desire for exact change. She sighed in relief; anticipating her programming, she had put it into her back pocket. She fished it out and slapped it on the table. She was tense and shook slightly. A slurp of insipid coffee—too watery to provide the necessary mood alteration—at least gave her time to take stock of events.

As Audrey consumed her sub, she pondered the irony of her situation. Her entire professional life had been a celebration of the mechanical perfection and uniformity of Canadian currency. While she was fully aware of the economic benefits, the coin in front of her was, really, an affront to her philosophical affiliation, worship almost, of coinage. Furthermore, it was technically a criminal offence to exchange the coin for its monetary value— that's how it had become so valuable. Though no one was likely to know of the incident without extensive research, she was violating an allegiance she placed above any in her life.

Nevertheless, it would be easy to do. She knew the exact person who would be able to set her up. Raj was the head of her local chapter of the Numismatic Alliance. He always had his finger in many pies, and would certainly know interested parties and handle the transaction. And as they both knew how valuable the coin was, she knew he wouldn't try to cheat her. Obviously he would need a bit of a commission, and she could see her way to that.

She tended to this business first. Raj was away from his desk at Trotter and Morgan. She left a message explaining events, and instructed him to be at the bank in an hour. Finishing off her celebratory sub, she then decided to call Vincent. After eight rings, he answered.

"Vincent, why don't you pick up the phone? It could be an emergency!"

"I—er, sorry ..." warbled across the receiver. Vincent worked as a firefighter, but Audrey knew he was rarely busy. "What is it anyway? You never call me in the middle of the day."

Audrey paused. "I've got something to celebrate. Why don't we go out tonight? Or we could stay in and I could open that bottle of sparkling white wine we got last Christmas."

Vincent mumbled affirmatively, said he would meet her in the bank at five, and hung up. Audrey had made up her mind, and strode out of the café with a steely determination in her eyes. To be safe, she held the penny at the centre of her white-knuckle clenched fist.

Audrey miscalculated her route back. Turning left outside the alley, she forgot the bank was on her left opposite the Currency Exchange. She usually approached it from the other side, to avoid the menacing offence to her professional ethics now lying despondently on the street a few yards in front of her.

The grey overcoat, frayed and flecked with unidentifiable grime, lay draped over an emaciated form, fingerless gloves and mottled shoes poking out from it. Dry hands listlessly played across a warped guitar. A cracked and angry voice belted out meaningless sounds. Around him, a few strips of canvas and cardboard had been erected, with numerous anti-government slogans and a strange limerick with a Latin punch-line. No one who walked by heeded him, other than to charitably drop their lunch change into his guitar case-cum-library.

This homeless man was once Employee of the Month Elgin Duchesne. He never really fit into the bank, and rarely spoke to his fellow employees. Nevertheless, Mr. Griffin had a soft spot for Duchesne. He made him Employee of the Month six times— roughly equivalent to every other employee, barring new acolytes. Mr. Griffin put down his equanimity to laziness: he frequently announced the Employee of the Month with his characteristic giggle, adding, "I always forget about this. Let's see ..." His chubby index finger would scan the room and pick the winner. While Audrey's respect for Mr. Griffin was in-built, she fumed at her co-workers' blasé acceptance of this random awarding process. The sixth time Duchesne received the award, she voiced her concerns to Mr. Griffin.

"Sweetheart, what are you worried about?" He always addressed his female employees as "sweetheart", but no one considered it chauvinistic as he called the men "sweetheart" as well. "Everybody wins, and it doesn't create that nasty competition in the workplace."

"But that's the whole point, sir!" she replied, trying to rein in her hysteria.

"Come here." He gestured for her to cross the desk and stand next to him. The third time she relented, and he pointed to a picture of a gormless-looking boy.

"That's my son. Most useless creature on the planet. Isn't smart, has no grace, and from what I know, he can't even brush his teeth properly. And he's thirteen. It's possible he may have absolutely no function in society. But I'm there for him, and I'm committed to him. He is more inherently valuable as a human being than this bank and every single procedure we have. So why care so much?"

Audrey found the lecture distasteful, and was uncomfortable with Mr. Griffin's personal titbits—his penchant for mooning opposing teams at football games, his bizarre anniversary presents (last year he hired an orchestra to play 'their' song, "Hip to be Square" by Huey Lewis and the News), and his habit of wearing the same casual pants and rolled-up, creased shirt for weeks on end.

Audrey determined to prove that she was more valuable than other employees. To this end she rigged her computer so that after her shift it would drop the decimal points from every transaction. At her second shift, she would "correct" the error, proving by noticing it that she was better than her colleagues.

Unfortunately, Elgin Duchesne needed the extra shift to take a flex day off. He hadn't discussed this with her, and she was unable to persuade him to leave his post. As a result, he discovered the error, but didn't know how to fix it. He assumed he had made a mistake, but voiced his suspicion that the only sensible explanation was that another employee had rigged the computers. He devoted weeks to investigating the matter. He seemed on the verge of figuring it out, but then abruptly quit one day.

It was difficult to tell what had happened, but it was obvious to Audrey that the incident had triggered a large-scale nervous breakdown and moral decay. He would sing and shout in the streets, "It's not fair!" He chose as his squat a place strategically near the bank, and everyone at the bank said he looked 'dead inside'.

Audrey chose not to think about him, and altered her route into the bank to avoid encountering him. This time, she increased her walking pace, a few coins contemptuously dribbling from her hand as she sped past.

Raj loomed over the front desk. He was talking to Grolsch, who looked rather annoyed at his conversation. Or maybe he was leaning back because he couldn't adjust the seat-tilt.

"Anyway, she said … oh, here she is now. Well, it was good talking to you." Grolsch nodded, and returned with relief to his computer. Raj strode over to Audrey, and she led him into a nearby office.

"When I heard your message, I flipped. I had to get over here. I mean, the Anarchist penny—do you have any idea--?"

"Five hundred thousand," Audrey interrupted. He may have been slightly disappointed at her excellent memory, but he continued beaming.

"That's a conservative estimate," he stated. "It could easily be double that. Well, no sense talking all day. Let's see the goods."

Audrey confidently reached into her pocket, and pulled out the penny. Raj's smug expression crumpled into annoyance. "Nice try, Audrey."

Audrey looked down, and was paralysed. The Queen's unblemished profile greeted her horrified gaze. Then, suddenly, she realised. As a mark of her disapproval, she always gave pennies to homeless people. As she had been so disoriented when she passed Elgin, she must have … she couldn't even think it. She was unable to speak, and simply stood up and staggered past Raj, out of the bank and onto the street. Duchesne was nowhere to be seen.

Vincent arrived at the bank, quizzically regarding the bustle around him. He rarely visited Audrey at work, and his most recent arrival was for a fire when the Bank Association visited. Audrey walked up to meet him, her normally blank face lined with worrying ambivalence.

"Hello, dear," Vincent said lamely. "Everything all right?"

She sighed, and smiled. A genuine smile was unusual for Audrey: a thin upraised mouth was her limit.

"I think…" she replied slowly. "I think I'm going to resign as treasurer of the Numismatic Alliance."

"Oh." Vincent wasn't sure how she wanted him to respond. He couldn't help but be relieved. She could spend up to three weeks every quarter obsessing over the accounts, and often used it as an excuse to shout at him. "Well … where did you want to go?"

That evening, following a day even less absorbing than usual, R.J. Simkins stopped by Joe's Cup of Joe. After his frustrating day, perhaps a cup of coffee and a bowl of chilli might soothe him.

He passed by a quickly exiting man in a shabby grey overcoat. He walked up to the desk and made his order. He cursed silently; he didn't have the exact change, leading to yet more pennies being dispensed.

As the cashier handed the change over, he paused for a minute. "Hey, look at that. There's something wrong with that penny." Simkins observed that the penny was very unusual: a hole in the Queen's temple and a squiggly moustache on the side. "You should hold on to it. Might be worth something."

Simkins paused a minute, and regarded the penny with a chuckle. After his day, that would be something. But he thought no more of it, and dropped the penny, along with the rest of his change, into the tip jar.

"I'm making it a policy to give away every penny I receive," he explained. "Otherwise I'll never change."

"You sure about that?" called a voice from the corner of the shop. Simkins looked across and saw the man in the overcoat was still standing in the doorway. He smiled, and Simkins smiled back at him rather madly.

"Tell you what, sir," offered Simkins, picking up the coin. "How about we flip for it?"

Hamish Crawford

The Empty-Headed Architect

Being a reprint of the reminiscences of Simba, Gentleman Adventurer

It was an unusually warm autumn day that led me to reflect on the phenomenon of flip-flops. As I passed numerous bystanders, their bare feet lazily smacking dirtied rubber platforms, it occurred to me that flip-flops are a singularly ugly garment. The design fails even on functionality—it throws into sharp relief the wearer's hairy or pasty foot, and its tenuous grip on the foot necessitates the wearer to adopt a gut-protruding saunter akin to a Neanderthal who'd really let himself go. Black, white, patterned, or merely a gaudy primary colour, one is left staring at a monument to fashion banality. As I gazed down at my shiny new Chelsea boots, I became fully aware of the loneliness of my position as a phaeton of fashion.

This flip-flop-related digression had distracted me from my task here: I, Simba, gentleman adventurer, was summoned away from my afternoon game of tiddlywinks by my good friend and colleague Dr. Carroll Osborne. Her message on the phone— "There's something very peculiar happening at Mapleton"— catapulted me from my armchair to the wheel of my Citroen 2CV, where I raced the 375cc flat-two engine into top speed while consuming the symphony of nougat, caramel, peanuts and chocolate that is the modern Snickers bar. Indeed, so enraptured was I with my car and chocolate that I missed the exit to Mapleton no fewer than three times. But here I was, and, having passed the previously mentioned scantily clad foot-masochists, I ran into Carroll. Though a flaxen-haired "English rose"-type beauty, Carroll frequently had an angry look on her face that gave her the air of a stern schoolteacher. I don't know why she gets so angry, and frankly feel that life's too short.

"Thanks for rushing down here, Simba, I've only been waiting an hour."

(As a side note, Carroll's complaining is subject enough for an entire book! Maybe one day…)

"Oh really Carroll, I had some difficulty finding the place." I would have mentioned the Snickers, but I somehow knew she wouldn't understand. We made our way past the village fair, traipsed through some wonderfully crunchy autumn leaves, and walked into the local hospital.

"The local doctors are baffled by it, and frankly, so am I."

"I know, but some people can't find shoes that fit them, and we must embrace people's right to choose whatever footwear they desire, no matter how much an eyesore."

"Simba, I don't know what you're talking about, but just come here and look at this man. His name's Fred Spinrad, a local architect." In a special roped-off wing lay a ragged-looking fellow, with an unkempt beard and a crazed expression. Carroll demonstrated her problem by producing an EKG. "Even a coma registers more neural activity than this."

The man suddenly blurted out, "Berry … Doctor Berry …"

Carroll looked sideways at me. "That's all he says. There's a Doctor Max Berry who lives up the hill. I called him earlier, but no one answered."

"Then it's time for a house call," I replied. "Max Berry— sounds like an energy drink." On that ominous note, we prepared to visit this mysterious figure.

*****

Doctor Berry's house was singularly devoid of cherry blossoms, orchards, or other fruity things that might be expected of a man with his name. Indeed, the gnarled branches twisting their way around the manor's stonework appeared deader than the surroundings. As the Citroen crept up the driveway, a chill blew through the air that added to my foreboding. Even the strains of "It's My Party and I'll Cry if I Want To" on my radio overflowed with incipient gloom.

Doctor Berry swiftly showed us into a plush drawing room. He was an ascetic-looking individual of about fifty, dressed in dusty tweeds. *Amazing that some people walk around in such outdated garb*, I mused as I stroked the quilted elbow patch on my crimson velvet smoking jacket. But I suppose we can't all be arbiters of sartorial excellence.

"Please sit down, Doctor Osborne, Simba," he said without warmth. After Carroll briefly explained our purpose, he added, "I understand the urgency of your inquiry, but I can't really help very much. I've only met this man Fred once, and I've been busy with my researches."

"And what researches would those be?" I asked pointedly.

"Oh, just a paper on a new way of looking at string theory. I haven't seen anyone but the milkman for the past month."

"And this milkman's name?" I shot back. I wasn't about to let Berry get away with anything. Carroll, an expert on many areas, glanced through the stacks of paper burying Berry's desk. She nodded approvingly at the scrawled reams of equations and diagrams that could have been written in Cyrillic for all that I understood of them.

"You've done some outstanding work here, Doctor Berry. Particle physics, neurology, history of Cthulhu worship[13], and … architecture?" She raised her eyebrow, and I remembered Fred. This was beginning to look suspicious.

"Well, I'm a firm believer that only through learning many differing disciplines can we become truly educated. That poor fellow, Fred, was an architect, wasn't he? I didn't know him very well. He knew I—er, *I* knew *he* was an expert, and I always like to talk to experts in every field."

As he spoke he followed my path across the room intently. There were six model brains mounted on desks and shelves around the room, each with copious notes, compasses, and diagrams. "Forgive me for mentioning it, Doctor Berry," I piped up, "but you have a singular interest in brains. Dare I ask, 'What's on your mind?'" My chuckles echoed mockingly, but such was the fate of my one-liners that only I appreciated their brilliance.

"Fascinating organ, Simba," he replied, his eyes burning. As he looked at me, I was certain there was a predatory interest. Pointing at the grey coils all across the model, he continued, "We are all so certain that our minds are telling us what's going on. But by stimulating different neurons, one can create reactions that give subjects false impressions. That one there, for instance, and you would insist you could hear loud music even in utter silence. The most minute physical alteration, and the certainties of the world around us come crumbling down." He said nothing, his vulpine gaze penetrating me.

"Er … jolly good," I croaked. I looked imploringly over at Carroll, but she just rolled her eyes.

Thankfully, this awkward moment was interrupted by a high-pitched zap. As Doctor Berry and I ducked, a beam of light shot above us. Looking over at the door, we saw a dark-haired, slender woman holding some kind of large box with a long tube attachment—something between a laser gun and a vacuum cleaner. We all froze for a minute, in that way when both sides suddenly become aware that they're looking at each other. While in social situations this yields a bashful apology and an awkward catch-up conversation, in this case the stranger darted away from the window. Carroll and I dashed off after her.

The state of decay was evident behind the house, where misshapen trees writhed in tableaux of expressionistic agony. Coming up to the charming wrought-iron warriors' gate, I realised to my dismay that I had come full circle. In the distance I spotted the woman, but the light was failing, and I leapt forward, landing right on top of her and sending us both tumbling down a ravine, the piles of leaves breaking our fall.

"Madam, forgive me for that, but I need to ask you a few questions and—" Her eyes widened with rage, and she opened her mouth, but no words came out. I reached out to lend her a hand, but she punched me. I flailed out as I fell backwards, and by pure chance grabbed the box she was carrying. She ran off into the distance, and I was left looking like a clumsy clot.

Carroll came running after me. "Yes, yes, she got away," I grumbled.

"Are you all right?" she asked. I showed her the device, and her eyes narrowed. We returned inside, to see Berry unconscious. I was somewhat alarmed, but Carroll calmly knelt at his side and touched the tube to his head. "Just as I thought—I'm reading neural activity from three separate brains."

I was getting increasingly baffled. "Fred the architect and who else?"

Carroll and I dashed off after her.

"Her," Carroll replied. "I met her once. That's Doctor Nina Ellroy. She couldn't speak, could she?" I nodded. "She tried to fire that beam at Berry. She and Fred were left with immediate residual memories only—she came back here for the same reason Fred was saying one name over and over. I think Doctor Berry's developed a way to steal minds."

Another thought occurred to me. "This is changing the subject, but two doctors in one neighbourhood, eh? Guess this is the place to get a broken ankle!" I chortled.

We stayed until Doctor Berry regained consciousness, but barring offering him a reviving brandy, our conversation with the chap was guarded. After all, he had two surplus minds lurking in that dome-shaped skull. I'd taken particular care to hide the brain-box under the dog blanket in my Citroen, and Carroll insisted that I mention neither it nor Doctor Nina Ellroy. Then, as we were walking out the door, Carroll arranged to meet him at the Mapleton Players' gala performance of *Faust* that evening.

As we drove back to the town, I attacked Carroll with some frank words. "Great Googly-Moogly Carroll! Why the blazes did we agree to go to *Faust* with that man? First of all, we should confront the bounder now and get it over with. Secondly, I like opera as much as the next fellow, but three hours in the company of Gounod is the last thing I need after this exertion."

"Simba, don't you see? We'll bring Fred, and I'm sure Nina will show up by herself. The transfer evidently wasn't totally successful, as she was able to steal the device and follow Berry. But once they're there, we can reverse the controls and restore everyone's minds to their rightful bodies!"

After a refreshing Singapore Sling at the local public house, Carroll and I drove over to the Mapleton Opera House. There was some excitement that local Member of Parliament, R—b A—s[14], was in attendance. He was apparently a 'very right-wing Conservative', an obscure party bafflingly popular in these parts. And typically, my seat was right next to his. So I decided to at least be pleasant to this man.

"Good evening," I began. He uttered a bestial grunt in reply. I panicked, and leapt to my feet. "Carroll! It's another one! This A—s fellow has had his mind drained!" I was then taken aside and informed that this was how he communicated[15]. Whoops!

As Faust's tragic tale unfolded, the low lighting and my Singapore Sling made me suddenly weary. Typically, though, A—s was hogging the whole armrest, so every time my head drooped, I fell into his ample shoulders. And every time, an unhappy grunt signalled my error. In my battle to stay awake, I noticed Berry was becoming increasingly nervous as the opera progressed. His brow was slick with perspiration and he kept looking around his shoulder. Following his glances, I looked up at the balcony, where Nina stood glaring down at him.

Suddenly, he bolted from his seat and ran for the exit, and we were fractionally behind him. Thankfully Carroll was right on the aisle. Believe me, there is nothing worse than hurriedly shuffling past frowning opera patrons. I tell you, Krakatoa could be erupting and they'd still purse their lips if you left before the act break!

As Carroll ran to grab the machine from the coat-check guy, I followed Nina out the side door. Luckily, I had just the gadget for the occasion: a handy grappling hook piton gun. I fired the piton and swiftly glided up the stairs. Offering silent thanks to Batman, patron saint of grappling hooks, I hopped over the rail and jumped at Nina. She ran backwards and out into the lobby. "Wait! I'm on your side!" I called out. I pushed past a rather angry team of ushers with a cry of "Don't let her get away!"

On the mezzanine floor, Nina and I came face to face with Carroll, Berry, and I think Fred was standing by the espresso bar. "Quickly Carroll! They're all here!"

"Don't do it!" Berry cried. But Carroll twisted the lever, and with an almighty whoosh and some lights, everyone seemed restored to normal.

"You did it!" a husky feminine voice exclaimed.

"Sorry I took so long," Carroll replied. "Good to have you back, Doctor Ellroy."

Nina turned to Berry, the full angry fire in her eyes. "I can't believe you, Max. I tell you that machine's dangerous, and you try to steal my brain? And the credit!"

Berry scowled back at her. "Typical of you, Nina, you never could see the big picture. And what dangers? I survived having you and Fred inside my head, didn't I?"

"Yeah, but it wasn't much fun!" Fred piped up. Nina nodded.

"I hate to break up the reunion," I interrupted, "but what exactly is *that*?" The machine had discharged a creature fouler than my worst imaginings. It resembled a squid, but had at least twenty eyes, and a mixture of scales and feelers dotted across its rubbery carapace. It slithered towards us, making a grotesque, bilious gurgling sound.

"That's what I'd worried about!" Nina shouted. "It's the sum total of our negative mental energy—Berry's, mine, Fred's. It's only going to get worse. Carroll, quickly, turn the machine to maximum."

Carroll complied, but turning up the controls only caused strange static shocks to bounce off its carapace.

"A puny … effort," it croaked sarcastically[16].

But in a flash, a thought came to me. "Quick, everyone—through here!" We all ran through a side door, the creature rolling in a kind of blobby lope after us. Unfortunately, the door led directly onto the stage, and I was nearly floored by the filthy glare I got from the tenor whose aria we interrupted. And the clot didn't seem half as irritated by the monstrosity trundling in behind us.

"Uh, Simba—explanation?" Carroll plaintively asked.

"I thought we might refer this to an elected representative," I archly replied. Exactly as I had hoped, A—s and the creature locked eyes, and in an almighty buzz of energy, the creature disappeared. A—s, however, stood in the middle, and grunted triumphantly. Everyone stood and gave a round of applause.

"Well, it was nothing," I airily said, waving off the acclaim.

"I hate to say it," Nina said, "but I think they're applauding him."

And indeed the ingrates were, as the cries poured out, "Hooray R—b! What a great guy!"[17] He bowed vainly. I rolled my eyes, on my behalf and Gounod's.

*****

With Dr. Berry in the care of the Direw University Peer Review Committee[18], we all retreated to the Frogspawn's Arms for a much-needed drink.

"Well, I think you did very well, Simba," Carroll opined, patting me on the shoulder. I admit her approval was a welcome balm in the absence of more widespread acclaim.

Nina turned to me, trying to work it all out. "So, knowing A—s was famously empty-headed, his brain would be the only one that could contain a creature that fed on minds for its sustenance?"

"Er… something like that, I think." I had to admit my precise train of thought seemed to have jumped tracks somewhere, but that kind of summed it up.

Fred turned to Nina. "What I want to know is why did Berry want our minds so much? One second, he was telling me how much he liked my book, the next, well, indescribable weirdness."

Nina was blunt in her assessment. "He was always competitive, and irrationally hated anyone who was better at anything than him. So what could be better than absorbing their talents for his own purposes?"

"With that in mind Nina, I hope you've destroyed that machine," Carroll inquired, with head-girl primness.

"Yes, of course, Carroll. In fact, what do you say to an inter-disciplinary study of anthropology and telepathy, from a cultural-history perspective?"

"Interesting idea," Carroll mused. "What are your initial thoughts?"

"Ladies, might I suggest another round of libations, and perhaps some hearty steak pies?" In response to their blank stares, I simply said, with a twinkle: "You know—brain food!"

No good?

Hamish Crawford

This Particular Band

Of course I love this particular band. That was common in the 1960s, and people often begin similar recollections by saying "Everyone of my generation knows what this particular band means." But I'm not of that generation, I come from one of the later ones. For us, the music has lingered on. It's unaccountably still here, and every bit as alive as it was the day it was recorded. Many find that frustrating, and make a big showy point of not liking them. After all, they say, it's our dads' music, old news; let's get on with the new stuff.

But there comes a point when you can't ignore this particular band. There's the pointless Shakespeare comparison— pointless because it's true. No one likes being told what to like, and for the last four hundred-odd years everyone (except Joan Collins, maybe) sings the praises of the Bard. So it's a fact. Shakespeare is a genius, *ipso facto*. Aesthetic taste shouldn't be a fact, but in the two wonky cases of Shakespeare and this particular band (if no others, thank God), it somehow is.

I won't bore you by saying which album is my favourite. I suppose I couldn't even if I wanted to. There's just as much to love about their earliest, most insignificant bubblegum pop as there is about their later stuff.

Then about '67 they push every boundary going—and again, here's the boring part where I have to mention drugs. They were on drugs, you have to be on drugs to fully appreciate this. I don't know; I do know that they made a brilliant album under influences that caused many, many other bands to turn out meaningless, self-indulgent drivel. See, *everyone* took drugs; not everyone made profound, evocative music. Music that causes people who weren't even born at the time get a taste of that era, the full flavour of the freedom and the joy. That's more mind-bending than drugs.

Put it this way. When I put on any of their songs, I can just see a sunny, glorious summer's day in England in 1967. More than that, actually; I can walk around in that never-never land, for those handful of minutes. There's a particular one that I identify with the final episode of *The Prisoner* (guess which one) broadcast in February 1968. I suspect even if I had lived through it all, been in those places, I would still get the same picture. I wonder how people's mental images differ; does everyone look back and imagining the same idyll.

But I liked it all; even their last album, which some friends with better judgement say was getting self-indulgent, is utter genius. Their most banal song (and all right, they had a few banal ones in their time) will still have something special, something utterly cherishable about it.

People are always asked who their favourite member was. Sadly, they too (or rather, they four) have become stuck into their own boxes, each as broad and doubtless inaccurate as a cartoon. He was the genius, he was the nice guy, he was the quiet one (whose understated brilliance never got him the recognition he deserved). And him on the end? Well, some people think he's a bit of a joke. But that's not fair; it's inevitable that such special people will have a pecking order, but I don't think he would argue that he was anything special. He just seems to have enjoyed being with the others.

Then again, I probably wouldn't know. In that vague, nebulous way everyone knows about pop culture, I'm aware of the orthodoxies, and how my opinions tally with them. I never read any of the retrospective writing, I haven't looked up any of the reviews at the time. I haven't picked up any of today's leading music journals to see what the big hitters of today think I should find particularly brilliant about these guys. Nostalgia seems to fuel it all, and while I'm as nostalgic as the next person, as an industry it can get a bit cynical, a bit chokeed in its own dust. I'd rather just listen to the songs; it's far more fun. It does, however, mean I don't know much about the people, except the snippets I've been told by friends who are experts.

I have a feeling that the people themselves might have been slightly less than their myths. I doubt any human being could inhabit myths of that size. It's slightly disappointing to imagine them consumed by petty human concerns. And they undoubtedly were: money and sex and drugs and success and vanity and envy seem to encrust themselves, unwanted, around the mythos. A few years into their solo lives they very probably lived rather boring lives (save for their more ostentatious demonstrations). Two of them who live to this day undoubtedly do; some of their greatest fans seethe with resentment that they continue to live nicely but not *do* much. What little output they can manage is immediately resented—a few concerts and a new—almost totally inoffensive and unmemorable—album every so often.

So I love, but I don't know. But I do have some idea of how much they meant to so many. I've felt the same myself. And anyway, there's no way you can avoid it. There doesn't seem to be anyone who doesn't have some connection, some story, an opinion. As more cynical decades have come and gone, it's harder to conceive how connected to them everyone felt; and how much love there was. People from all walks of life seemed to respond to them somehow. The purity and spread of that love is almost inconceivable from a distance of forty years.

I followed everyone's careers afterwards, and know the same sad details everyone else does. Grief seems to linger in people's minds more than happiness. But even when that terrible day, the worst imaginable fate happened to him, in among those bitter, grey tears, and that bitter grey time, there were tiny little rays, tiny little memories of better days fifteen or twenty years ago. In that coldest and bleakest of winters, those brief snatches must have glowed like the purest sunshine.

But here's a weird thing: there are the hundreds of movies and books and writing and thinking about that era—it continues to fascinate and stimulate, so long afterwards. But you'll never find these songs, these people, this music—which played such a large part in that whole ethos.

Oh, I know there are a few wildcat exceptions. But there's something very important to bear in mind about those exceptions. They're all the result of long phone calls and negotiations, and a lot of people in suits have spent long hours arguing about them. And finally, a lot of people (including, yes, those two who aren't doing much else) will pick up rather large cheques.

You might say that's only fair and proper. I don't object to the principle. The *level* it's enforced is sad, though.

But for such perfect music—it moves so many, it's so technically advanced it would be a mind-blowing soundtrack to any film—it's sad that it sits behind desks, locked away and hoarded. It should be out there, but it seldom is. How could it be? No one can afford it, so it stays locked up.

I guess at the end of the day it doesn't really hurt anyone. People still enjoy it, people in droves still ramble on about it, so what's the loss?

But in another respect, it's the pettiest indignity of all. No worse than that, it's sacrilegious.

There isn't much held to be sacred in this day and age. Perhaps if Johann Sebastian Bach's opuscula were the subject of legal wrangling the criminality of it would be more apparent.

So, as you may have guessed, that's why I haven't told you who I'm talking about. I mean, I could have, I suppose. I too could pick up my phone, ask permission, send my gushing in to the official channels, who would probably (hopefully) have no particular problem with it. I would then go back and duly insert all the names and songs and everything would be above board.

I don't think I will. Paradoxically, perversely even, it means too much to me. Too much, certainly, to be reduced to the crude money-spinning business it seems no more than to some people. So they must remain this particular band, the singers and songs anonymous.

It doesn't seem right. It just doesn't.

But you know it's *them*.

Lightning In a Bottle

The car is naturally out of control. I knew from the moment I got in that something would go wrong, but I just couldn't figure out what. It was only a matter of time. Everyone in the car agrees; I catch the two guys in the back seat looking worryingly at me. Then again, they worry about everything, so maybe their testimonials weren't very reliable. Of course, I know she didn't think anything could go wrong. My tirades about modern car safety and car accident frequency always fall on deaf ears. Stubborn to the last, she remains quiet even now.

Typical; she would rather die than admit that I was right.

I can't even see out the window. Everything's blurred into a cacophony of blinding light. I think I can make out people's faces, staring at me in a mixture of pity and horrified interest, making a grim spectacle of my last moments. Struggling to move my inert body, I catch a brief glance of the dials on this so-called family car. I didn't even think the needle went that far down the speedometer. However, seeing as the maximum speed (which they marked so helpfully on the dashboard, never expecting you to actually reach it) was 180 km/h, I would have to estimate the current speed being around 220. Even assuming I could reach the brake pedal with my useless leg, we'd be dead anyway.

Now, the indistinct images clear up, and form a solid cement wall. The car that I find myself unable to pilot is careening into the wall. I'm trying to overcome the panic, to find some way out of this. I could grab control of the wheel and get us out of this collision course. But it wouldn't be much use anyway; we seem to have veered into some kind of one-way alley. At least a crafty sidestep might speed up the inevitable impact, and maybe reduce the damage.

No good. The wall still bears down on us. I catch one last glimpse of her, her smooth, beautiful face. She's the one I really feel sorry for. So much I couldn't say. Still, we're both done for now, so I suppose I won't—

The final, sudden crash comes so quickly I almost miss it. I expect it to hurt more than it actually does, but that's a mistake I'm always making. As life pours away from my body, I take solace in the fact that I've died with her.

The men surveyed the wreck with grim, clinical dispassion. They weren't doctors, after all; they just carefully noted any damage sustained, ticked off the problems peculiar to this specific car, and carried on. Theirs was a profession dedicated to reporting and cataloguing destruction, reducing wreckage and ruin into happy red check-marks or disgruntled 'X's in a notebook sheet, and from there, onto graphs and analysis charts.

Jeremy weaved past them, somewhat disgusted by their fascination with the transformation from gleaming, German-constructed chariot of efficiency into useless heap of metal, rubber, and walnut burr panelling. Jeremy rushed over to the four bodies that lay buried amid the rubble.

He would do what he could for the victims. That was his job. When he started out, he would never have thought he'd be hit so hard by these accidents. But over the last six months, seeing the repeated melees saddened him. His co-workers clearly thought he was soft, and Jeremy suspected they were right. Was it crazy to be soft, though? Should someone take all this mayhem in his stride, just because it's part of his routine? Jeremy didn't like his co-workers anyway, and was content to let them look sideways at him while he focussed on his work.

He wondered where the attitude came from. Part of it was when he saw the same faces behind the wheel. He shook his head when he saw the driver. This was the third accident this guy had been involved in this month. He picked up the inert body, and somehow sensed the pain he had gone through. That pain made Jeremy's task so much more difficult.

Somehow Jeremy would get this poor soul back into shape, so that he could be sent out on the same suicide mission again.

I'm awake now. I see the man staring at me, smiling down at me, pleased with his handiwork. The guy looks familiar… Jeremy, that's it. He's the guy who looked after me the last couple of times I've been in here.

I cast my eyes down to look at my limbs. I don't know how Jeremy did it, but everything is in perfect working order. They're still a bit tender from the operations, so I decide not to do any jumping jacks right away. But even without moving, I can feel the tingling buzz of life in my body.

"Pretty amazing, isn't it buddy?" Jeremy asks. I gesture that he's done a good job, but I can't speak yet, and he knows it. "I know you appreciate what I do."

I don't like admitting it, but I'm almost a regular in this place. Hell, I'm on first name terms with the guy, and likewise, he is with me.

"Arty," he chuckles. "Of all the guys I get in here, I have to say you're my favourite. It's weird, I know, but it's true. I tell you, it gets lonely as hell in here. These guys wouldn't know the difference between a person and a titanium cantilever unless one or the other hit them in the head." He sighs. "Sometimes I feel like you're the only guy who listens."

He chuckles again, nervously this time. All the other people around the ward—doctors, nurses, and hospital staff, I guess—stare at him as he does this. He scowls back at them. Of course, none of them have the personal touch. Whenever one of them handles me it feels like I'm just a piece of meat. But Jeremy—he knows how to treat a guy.

I nod again, and try to wrench my mouth into a smile. He understands what I mean.

"Now, you try to stay out of trouble, Arty," he concludes, patting me gently on the head. "The last thing I want to do is see you in here again."

I'd like to get to know Jeremy better. I really appreciate the care he's given me. But I get the feeling there's more to him than the nice-guy exterior. I'm an expert at body language, and he's obviously a bit of a loner. I'm kind of an expert on body language, and I can read those glances everyone gives him. But why's he so friendly to me, then? What have I done to deserve his special treatment?

The technicians burst in again. God, they're everywhere these days. I can tell they're talking about me. Jeremy looks back at me for just long enough to confirm that I'm the topic of conversation. It's also the kind of look that tells me they're not going to give me a two-week vacation to Bermuda.

"I'm sorry, but that's the way it is."

"Listen to me. I've just finished fixing him up, and now you want to use him again? He isn't ready, he won't survive."

"Jeremy, you're raising your voice. I'm worried that you're not handling this professionally."

Lawrence Hull, The man presently speaking to Jeremy, was a good two feet taller and wider than him. His lab coat was bursting at the seams to try to contain the very junior assistant's superfluous body. Nevertheless, his sheer bulk succeeded in making Jeremy feel intimidated, and considering his qualifications, he resented that. Then again, no one ever listened to Jeremy around here, so Lawrence's insubordination was predictable.

"Honestly, Jeremy, the tests have to be done. Whether that one does it, or one of the others, will it really make any difference? They're not going to last forever."

Jeremy felt there should have been something he could have said, some restriction that could have prevented them from taking poor old Arty out again. He smiled ruefully; in some ways it was his fault. He'd done such a good job getting Arty shipshape that they could use him as soon as they were ready for him.

Jeremy looked back at Arty, still recovering and lying, motionless but healthy, on the table. He looked back, and as soon as their eyes locked, Jeremy's head swivelled rapidly and painfully back, a reflex reaction to cover his guilt. Once again he levelled with his hierarchical inferior and weighty superior.

"Oh, all right then, take him away." Jeremy then unexpectedly grabbed the man's already bulging shirt, and pulled towards his face. The man was flabbier than his broad shoulders suggested, and Jeremy was surprised to see him cringing in terror. "You'd better make sure he gets back in one piece, all right?"

Jeremy was satisfied to see the man nod weakly. He pushed Lawrence away and headed to his office.

"Honestly, Jeremy," the man called back. "You really need to chill out." The only response was the slam of Jeremy's office door.

When I wake up, I'm being manhandled by two burly technicians. Damn, Jeremy mustn't have been able to stop them. I can hardly blame the guy; he's a good buddy, but he isn't exactly the most assertive individual. Again, it's body language; that fat guy pushes him around like he's the new kid at the office. But hey, I shouldn't be making snap judgements. The workplace atmosphere is more like a factory than a hospital.

I only had about thirty-six hours to recover from this crash, and I'm back in control of a car? I'd say these guys have a third-party death wish, but seeing as it's my life they're playing with, I didn't find the thought particularly funny.

I'm roughly thrown into the driver seat, then they fasten the seatbelt around my waist. Ah well, at least she might be here again.

What? Looking to my side, I can see it's some other person. He's a thin, weaselly type, and he keeps his mouth shut. That would have been all right normally—I've had my fair share of uncommunicative passengers, and usually it doesn't bother me. But now, we're both being stuffed into this cramped economy model sports car.

"So … you come here often?" I joke. No response, other than a scowl. Typical, I think; so much for trying to be friendly with people.

The run goes smoothly at first, and I feel like I've got the hang of the thing. Then the speed goes up again. Luckily though, we're not locked into a tunnel. Provided there's room to manoeuvre, I think I can handle this. Unfortunately, I realise that we now have a hulk of a van bearing down on us. A real freight train of a vehicle, face only a mom could love—a soccer mom, that is. I swerve left and right, but there's nothing I can do to avoid hitting the guy. Every turn my car makes, his car matches. The man's a complete idiot. Looking through the windows—and luckily we're at least going at a speed where I can see what I'm doing—my jaw almost hits the floor. She's in there! What the hell is she doing in a van with some other schmuck—less than two days after we both got out of hospital!

I'm enraged. So she just thinks she can play me for a fool? And now, I'm going to have to pay for her new squeeze's idiocy with my life!

Once again, I lose it. The wheels, the steering, the brakes, it all goes haywire. What kind of idiot makes these cars anyway? It seems to me like whenever something dangerous happens—exactly the kind of dangers that these cars are supposed to be tested against—you have no control of the thing and it ends up in disaster.

And that's exactly how it does end up. Guess Jeremy will be seeing me sooner than either of us would have thought.

I've spent slightly longer in the hospital this time: a total of two weeks under the insensitive floodlights and dry, sickly air. Jeremy isn't here to tend to me this time; I overheard in passing that he's asked to take some stress leave. I wasn't going to say anything, seeing as he did a great job on me last time, but I had noticed that his face was becoming increasingly lined, blemished with the vertical pock-marks of a man who desperately needed to chill out.

Unfortunately, this meant that for my two weeks' recuperation, I was looked after by those two imbecile interns, Julie and Craig. Hunched over the hospital television (blocking, I might add, my own view), it was all I could do to distract them away from their essential viewing: I implored them to switch over from *The Bachelor* to *Masterpiece Theatre*, but to no avail. And when they weren't watching it, they were yammering on about it: every time one indistinguishable slab of bland masculinity gets eliminated from the latest episode, they'd go into some lengthy debates over the merits of the contestants, invariably based on their bitchiness.

To be perfectly honest, it's a relief to be back on the road after having to put up with that pair. But now that I'm out, and thinking back on my recent history—well, things are starting to add up. I realise that I've been involved in no fewer than ninety-eight accidents in the last year. I can't believe this; I'd always thought I was such a responsible driver, and I keep trying to figure out why I'm losing control of my vehicle, and why these 'technician' guys keep deciding that I'm fit for another trip in my car. Surely that should be up to me to decide?

Anyway, now I'm behind the wheel of a hefty SUV; not my favourite car, but I've read that they get good safety reviews. Maybe I'll be able to avoid crashing this one. But this trip is made all the more memorable by the fact that she's back in the car. We exchange glances, and I just know that she's forgiven me for that last indiscretion (which, I'd heard, had completely obliterated the driver). Maybe, if I pilot this one well enough, I might be able to get away with her, and leave behind this rut my life has gotten itself stuck into: a seemingly endless round of car crashes and hospital visits, all under the auspices of these completely clueless—or maybe sadistic—technicians.

You see, I think I've figured out my mistakes. It's that even when I've thought I've been controlling the car, I haven't. It's those damn technicians. They control the speed and the direction the machine takes. Hell, I'm almost as much a passenger as my dear girlfriend (oh, all right, not a girlfriend yet, but you know what I mean…). But I think I've figured out a way to override this.

The car starts up. I'm driving steadily, I've got it all going on. This one's a different kettle of fish entirely. It seems like I'm driving through some kind of square. There are people all over the place, and I'm swerving to avoid them- or rather, these technicians are, and not very well.

But my plan goes into action. I'm able to animate my arms and legs. The effort is stupendous, but I now have my arms around the steering wheel and I'm actually turning the car the way I want it to go. I'm moving it back the other way along the track; I hear overhead alarms are going off. All of a sudden, I'm being surrounded by technicians. Well, I feel like telling them, it's my life and I'm going to take control of it at last! I'm able to wave my fist at them, and I feel good about it.

I kick open the door, grab her, and we barrel-roll out just as the Arctic silver behemoth swerves, completely on its own now, and plummets dully into the wall.

We're out now. I'm moving! I've just got to get off the road and into a nearby building. The effort is immense, and I drag her along. I look back, and I see that she isn't moving. I fear the worst, but she still seems to be alive. But damn it, she just *isn't* moving. I can't work out whether it's down to stubbornness or inability, but I know that I can't possibly leave her behind. She's my only hope.

"Come on," I grunt, heaving her along. "We've only got one chance."

But the effort is just too much. I collapse. My body just can't take the strain. That jump must have hurt me harder than my body seems to think. I can see Jeremy, off in the distance, looking nervous as always. My escape attempt has failed and I don't even know why. I think it's the fact that I've misjudged her so much that makes me feel the worst. I thought she was someone special.

Now I realise that she's just a dummy.

Jeremy stared down at Arty. He seemed to be all right, but there was something different, something Jeremy wasn't even sure if he quite believed. It seemed like the glimmer in those empty eye sockets had gone.

"I've never seen anything like it," Todd was saying to Andy, as they surveyed the still-standing SUV. "The technical failure was completely inexplicable. It was as if something just seized control of the thing."

"But what?" Andy replied. "It just doesn't make sense."

"And the other thing is, how did these two dummies end up outside the car like that? Every test we've done has concluded that from a frontal collision, it would be impossible for passengers to be thrown out at this angle, especially if they were wearing their seatbelts."

Andy looked up from inside the wrecked vehicle and scratched his head. "And what happened to the seatbelts? They're unclipped! Someone screwed up."

"There is one other possibility," Jeremy mused. He was talking to himself more than anyone else, but such was the gravity and sadness invested in his words that Todd and Andy couldn't help but listen. "They could have jumped."

Todd and Andy burst out laughing, and walked away, muttering, "I thought he was away on stress leave."

"Hey!" Jeremy called after them. "You guys are done? Don't you want to know how this happened?"

Andy shrugged airily. "Someone screwed up," he repeated.

"What's to know?" Todd asked. "I'll tell you something though. This is going to be *the* talking point of the *Consumer Digest* reports."

"If it makes it in," Andy added. "The guys upstairs are going to bust a gut over this."

They stood around aimlessly, staring at Jeremy. Jeremy looked back at them. Andy asked, "Uh, so… *was* there anything else?"

Jeremy rolled his eyes and looked down at Arty. "No … on you go." They hurried out, keen to file their reports and get away from Jeremy.

Jeremy bent down to pick Arty up, and suddenly found himself giving the inanimate creature a hug.

Sheila, his usually emotionless superior, walked in at this moment. Jeremy hadn't noticed until she walked over to him.

"I think that dummy's out for the count. We won't be able to use it again."

"Yeah, I know. Do you think I'll be able to take him home?" he asked.

Sheila stared quizzically at him, but didn't see why not. "He looks … sad, somehow, doesn't he?" she said, staring into the eyes.

"Yeah, he does. Poor old Arty, he was always a bit too emotional for this job, I thought."

"Arty?" she repeated, not understanding. She looked at the chest plate, and understanding dawned on her. "Oh, I get it. The model number—R.T.6785."

Jeremy chuckled, finally revealing his private joke, and remembering all those one-sided conversations. He picked up the R.T.7876 that lay beside him, first detaching their seemingly connected hands.

"May as well give him a girlfriend, eh?" Jeremy added.

"I don't know …" Sheila muttered, her voice trailing off. She was oddly disturbed by the image of 'Arty's hollow eye sockets. For a moment she though there was something in that dark recess, staring back at her with a burning intensity. She looked at his fellow dummy and was surprised to see no similar intensity. She looked across at Jeremy and shook her head. "I think we can still use the other one, but this one's finished. Sorry, buddy, you're on your own now."

"He's earned a rest," Jeremy smiled.

She turned back to Jeremy. "To be perfectly honest, all these dummies creep me out anyway."

"Yeah, well, maybe old Arty feels the same way about all these technicians."

Heat Wave

Calgary is a city whose heat is vengeful. After the icy depths of its winters, and even its springs, Calgarians expect payment in kind. Its inhabitants crave summer like addicts, and when it comes, it always seems to disappoint. Not for these discerning citizens are balmy summer days of twenty or twenty-two. If you are to pass people on the streets on those days, they will definitely tell you how they're still waiting for summer to start. And if Calgary has the audacity to offer rain? It's best to avoid talking to anyone—they silently shuffle from building to building, bundled up in overcoats, their scowls as grey as the overcast sky. It doesn't matter how many uninterrupted days of dry heat precede (or succeed it), rain is always unwelcome, undeserved.

However, for a few days in July and another handful around the end of August, the temperature soars. Finally those Calgary scowls turn into satisfied grins. Golf courses up and down the city fill up with hordes of businessmen, middle-managers and sundry oil-related jobsworths, keen to squeeze hard-earned enjoyment out of their days. Everyone finally seems content, and eager to…

What, exactly? Maurice Exline never actually knew. Today was August 14th, and it was thirty-two degrees Centigrade when he stepped out into Kensington. The last nine days had seen the temperature consistently hover in the infernal haze between twenty-eight and thirty-three. What, he wondered, do people *do* in this heat?

The morning had been unsatisfying. He showed up first thing at Mrs. Kosinski's wood-panelled palace in Mount Royal, keen to get into her regal garden and see the progress of the new flowers he was working on.

Maurice found gardening a difficult occupation in this city. In a good year, the skilled gardener could count on six months of growth—but with those freak late spring snowfalls, and the occasional autumnal temperature dip, that season could shrink to four. September began with full summer optimism, but ended shrouded in chilly gloom and piles of dead leaves.

The project in Mrs. Kosinski's garden, which Maurice had so far spent six weeks on, revealed another sobering truth. Even at the height of the growing season it was a true battle to keep plants alive. For July and August's parching, withering heights were less kind of plants than to people. Whereas the city's fauna could retreat to air-conditioned interior comforts when they were overcome, its flora had no such option, and had to endure the season's full infernal whimsy.

So far, Maurice had kept just ahead of the game. An ambitious planting regimen had kept the peonies, azaleas, and crocuses still looking fresh. However, the tulips he had introduced to the array had proved a little less hardy. This morning they drooped listlessly, the dirt beneath them like a simmering pie crust.

The tulips' progress wasn't helped when a drought warning late in June forbade watering plants. Maurice was so pained by the flowers' suffering that the day after he brought some smartly bottled name-brand water. He bought quite a few bottles over the week, and when it finished up more expensively than he had predicted, Mrs. Kosinski simply wrote it off as "Expenses". Maurice was certain she would have had a problem with it, and had even prepared a "You don't understand what it takes to keep your garden alive!" speech. Like many of the great speeches in his life, he never got a chance to give it because she was so accommodating. Her compassion and commitment to her garden was unexpectedly touching.

Mrs. Kosinski strode through her spacious lounge and into her spotless kitchen. Being inside, in the dark and mechanically cooled house was quite disorienting for Maurice. Even after he took off his glasses, Maurice's eyes strained to make out any shapes amid all the dark wood. He staggered through the hall, feeling his way along the corridor, and headed as quickly as possible to Mrs. Kosinski's deck.

"Good to see you again, Maurice." her voice's natural condescension extended to putting the emphasis on the first syllable of his name to make it sound like "More 'E's". She then asked if he would like some coffee, but her emphatic speech made it sound like a demand; so, even though a piping hot drink was the last thing Maurice wanted, he dutifully nodded and mumbled some thanks.

Her uncommonly muscular forearm heaved the urn and poured out a large mug-full of thick black liquid. She unceremoniously lunged it in Maurice's direction, and he gratefully accepted it and took a swig. Its dark colour and boiling temperature were misleading. The coffee was quite weak, and Maurice only drank a diplomatic quarter of the mug before sliding it onto the counter.

Maurice gazed out the back door longingly. He didn't feel comfortable in this cavernous house; its sombrely tasteful décor felt even more suffocating than the inferno outside. Also, the angle he was perched at for his casual lean against the counter was giving him acute back pain. He tried to move, but was frozen. The atmosphere of restraint and repression was getting to him. It was hardly helped by Mrs. Kosinski, who stared silently at him.

After the two stared ahead in silence for an eternal few seconds, Maurice, not being able to take the pain any longer, straightened himself out and, with a stretch of his arms, announced, "Well, I should really get out into that garden."

"Oh, yes, of course! You must indeed, More 'E's. If you don't tidy things up out there, my dear husband will wonder what I'm paying you for." She laughed gaily, and Maurice chuckled weakly as he walked outside.

As the sun seared his flesh, Maurice heard some pantomime-esque wheezing, and turned around to see Mrs. Kosinski waddling slowly out the screen door. She had lately been rather poorly, and abandoned her major summer project—a diet— having lost only seven pounds.

The sun cast an ochre prism around the garden. There was a faint aroma of burning in the air—possibly the legacy of forest fires, or the inevitable result of so many varnished decks crumbling.

A few loose floorboards made Maurice tip-toe off the patio and out to the flowers.

Mrs. Kosinski thrust her belly out, put her neck back, and drew in a lungful of air. She smiled. "What a gorgeous day!" she exclaimed.

Maurice nodded. He went to the tap and filled his buckets.

Mrs. Kosinski paced up and down the deck for a few minutes. Her breathing got slower and slower, and then she retreated back inside.

As Maurice started watering the flowers, the sun really started slicing through him. After five minutes his forehead was slick. Within twenty he was utterly drenched and feeling nauseous from the coffee, and even this minimal exertion had completely exhausted him. The air was thick with heat, and difficult to breathe in. He sat on a neglected swing-bench, thankfully shaded, while he refilled the jugs.

Maurice was wearing his lightest and thinnest clothes—a ragged long-sleeved cotton shirt over some old yellow overalls. Despite the temptation, he didn't want to be one of those workers who wore no shirt. As well as lingering self-consciousness about his beer belly, he hated all-over sunburn. His skin was naturally pasty, and a summer's work gave him an indifferent farmer's tan.

Maurice trudged across the charred blades of grass, past his successful flowers. The peonies' gigantic heads drooped, unsuccessfully supported by their spindly stalks. Near the back of the garden, the troublesome tulips wilted away, looking totally decrepit.

Maurice watered them. It was a difficult battle, to be sure; as much as they craved the water, if he gave them just a bit too much they would drown. The soil drank in the water, but the tulips still looked forlorn.

"Don't worry, guys," he said. When he started gardening, he had felt slightly self-conscious, and stupid, talking to the flowers—it seemed a pretty obvious badge of incurable eccentricity, as its connection with Prince Charles underlined. But as he had grown older, he found it pleasantly cathartic. Knowing his comments would definitely not be misunderstood freed Maurice to be more open and expressive than he ever was with a human. From dating woes to ideas for his oft-postponed doctoral thesis, Maurice's open-ended monologues were invariably the most satisfying. And at least he wasn't pretending that the flowers were actually responding to what he was saying. Although today, he thought just for a moment the miserable-looking tulips nodded their tightly sealed petals at him.

He looked around for a moment, and then tentatively stroked the skin of the nearest tulip. The flower was far drier than it looked, and the entire head disintegrated in his hand. Damn it! He hadn't been delicate enough!

He walked away stiffly, burning with anger at himself.

Maurice walked into the shed to get some more fertiliser. He rummaged through all three bags unsuccessfully. He then mentally ticked himself off for doing the same thing as he did at home with milk cartons—returning them to the fridge with a few paltry dredges sloshing around.

The flowers would need some today, so he would have to make an irritating trip to the local garden centre—no doubt he'd have to tangle with that man with the glass eye and permanent indigestion.

He walked back over to the house. When he had nearly gotten to the door, he jumped at the sound of Mrs. Kosinski shouting.

"What the hell do you think you're playing at?" she screamed.

Maurice was momentarily quite scared. She was a formidable woman and could almost certainly beat him in a physical fight. He turned his head slowly and cautiously, almost paralysed with anxiety.

He sighed; she was actually screaming at someone on the phone. As she shouted out accusations, pepped with a surprising array of expletives, Maurice shrank back. Even more surprising than the language was the emotion. Her face was contorted with pain and sorrow, and her eyes seemed completely lifeless.

Maurice was fascinated for a moment, but after that the anxiety crept back; Mrs. Kosinski was, after all, a strong-willed woman who would probably vent her frustration on the nearest subordinate to hand. Added to that, Maurice doubted she would appreciate being observed in such a sad and vulnerable state. He looked around, as though a search-light had picked him out. He retreated down the steps and walked around to the front of the house, and went to get his fertiliser.

To be on the safe side, Maurice bought four bags of fertiliser. And, as he predicted, he had to trade some barbed pleasantries with that strange glass-eyed man. On the way back from the garden supply store, Maurice went through all their encounters, struggling to find some reason, something he'd done to antagonise him. One thing was certain: his animosity grew each time they met.

"Nice weather out there, eh?" the man began, as he scanned the fertiliser.

"A bit too sunny for my taste," Maurice replied.

"Well, *I* wouldn't know. *I've* been stuck in here since eight this morning anyway." He gripped his stomach.

Maurice was eager to be on his way, but his debit card was doing a particularly involved "Processing…Dialling" routine; Maurice kept glancing down, hoping it may have dialled through. "Busy day?" Maurice had said to him.

"For *some* of us," he spat back. "Still working on Mrs. Kosinski's garden?"

"Yes," Maurice replied. "Oh, how did you know about that?"

"No, no, I get it." He waved his hand in angry dismissal. "Just because I work in a garden centre, I can't know anything about the people in Mount Royal?"

"No, I didn't mean that…" Maurice trailed off; nothing particularly pithy came to his mind, and it seemed that anything he said would only increase hostilities. His much-rehearsed speech putting the man down—which posed fascinating questions about where he got his attitude, who the hell he thought he was, and why he thought indigestion gave him the right to be such an insufferable, dictatorial martinet—would join its indefinitely-postponed fellows. And so he trailed off lamely, and stumbled out of the store without picking up his receipt. The glass-eyed man shook his head slowly and incomprehensibly as he left.

Maurice decided not to return straight away. It was now ten past one, and he still didn't know what the fall-out from Mrs. Kosinski's angry phone call might be. Not wanting to be on the receiving end, he decided to take a stroll in the direction of Kensington, and perhaps stop for a sandwich.

He decided to drop in on the coffee shop where his occasional girlfriend Lynn worked. Now in her second year of Humanities, Lynn had made herself over as a no-nonsense intellectual: severely cropped hair, rectangular glasses, and perpetual sangfroid. Not even her newfound austerity could disguise her natural beauty. No one looking at Maurice's blunter features would assume they were an item.

Since she started university, Maurice saw her only occasionally; he decided for her independence he should retreat from her life. He sorely missed her insights, and especially her unmatched way of telling him things he didn't particularly want to hear.

He filled her in on his most recent irritation. She was well versed in his ongoing feud with the glass-eyed man.

"I don't understand you, Maurice. Why do you keep going to that same garden centre, when every time you get so steamed up about this guy?"

"It's the nearest one to Mrs. Kosinski's house," he returned defensively.

She sighed. "It's the same with everything about your life. You stick yourself into corners so you have no alternative but to do something you hate, which you then complain about obsessively."

"That's not true," he said blandly. It wasn't the first time Lynn had offered a variation on this theory for Maurice's perpetual unhappiness.

"Well, then there's the fact that you hate people—but then, that's obvious from the gardening."

"What? What's wrong with gardening?"

"OK, I was just saying that to yank your chain. There's nothing wrong with gardening." She handed him his sandwich and a glass of water. Indicating the line, she shrugged apologetically. "Sorry, we'll pick this up later. Give me a call." Maurice gave a non-committal nod. With a cheeky smile, she added: "And enjoy the sunshine—I'm stuck inside."

Maurice made a face at her. She knew he hated days like this, but for some reason he enjoyed her needling.

As he sat outside, chewing his sandwich absently and taking lengthy gulps of ice water, Maurice thought over their brief conversation, and the oddball interactions that comprised his working life. He was certain that Lynn was wrong. He didn't hate people; he just found them so hard to understand and, frequently, not worth the effort.

Mrs. Kosinski was a perfect example. He enjoyed working for her. He certainly didn't dislike her, but he couldn't say he had a positive opinion of her either. He simply didn't know her, and in the absence of knowledge he found her ridiculous.

But suddenly she was harder to ridicule. For that second he had seen not just a superficial cavalcade of middle-aged eccentricities, but a fragile, possibly damaged person. And he didn't like the idea of dealing with that; he had no idea how, for one thing.

But then Lynn may have had a point about his other enmity. If he so hated exchanging barbs with that glass-eyed man, why the hell *did* he go to that particular garden centre? Did he just enjoy torturing himself?

Maurice returned to Mrs. Kosinski's house slightly after two. A cloud had granted him some brief respite, and he took the opportunity to water the remaining corners of the garden.

Hearing some movement behind one of the trees, Maurice stiffened. Obviously everyone around Mount Royal spent a lot of their time scaring their neighbours with tales of burglars, which he took as typical glass-house paranoia. He hardly knew what he'd do if he really confronted one, though. He knew he'd never have to worry about such an incident in his own house, a rented condo tucked away near Confederation Park. If he wasn't put off by the mouldy green eyesore pattern on the walls, any burglar worth his salt would take one look at the frayed furniture, the mismatched cups and cutlery, and the spotty carpet and move on rather quickly.

Ducking around the other side of the tree, he jumped when he saw it was Mrs. Kosinski. Hunched over and anxiously darting from right to left, she looked like she had shrunk. She appeared to have been wandering around for some time.

"Mrs. Kosinski?"

She jumped and spun around. "Oh, oh, More 'E's! There you are! I was looking for you! Where have you been?" She rattled her inquiries off in a frenzied babble.

Maurice was taken aback by her panic. He held up the fertiliser bags, and dumbly explained, "I, uh, just had to pop out and get some more."

"Oh, of course."

"Sorry I took so long."

She shook her head and held up her hand, trying to restore her haughty patina. "Silly of me. I just… wanted to talk about something…"

"Oh. What?"

She looked at him, and for a second he saw a glimmer of that earlier, haunted desperation. But she shook her head. "No, nothing. It's a bore. I won't burden you with it." She pulled out her chequebook. "How much do I owe you for the fertiliser?"

He shrugged, and explained that he'd forgotten to get a receipt. He almost started telling her about the glass-eyed man, but he was tired of hearing himself complain about it. She added forty dollars to his usual fee.

"Well, I suppose I'll be heading back inside." She turned away and slowly marched back to her house. She turned back and added, "You're doing a great job, by the way."

"Thank you, Mrs. Kosinski." She flashed him a disarmingly candid smile, and then walked away.

At the end of the day, as he did his final survey of the garden, Maurice was amazed to see that its healthiest-looking inhabitants were a handful of dandelions, and a few thistles. The weeds stood erect in the sunshine, as if staring smugly skyward, proud of their sturdy constitutions.

Maurice kept walking. Unlike all his fellow gardeners, Maurice had no particular problem with weeds. It certainly gave the garden a bit of character, and he personally thought it varied the otherwise bland topography of a manicured lawn. Every gardener he'd ever mentioned it to was quite offended by the concept. Like talking to flowers, or not scowling on a rainy day, such a viewpoint was generally considered incurably peculiar.

But curiously, Mrs. Kosinski never mentioned them. So Maurice was happy to let them enjoy the sunshine. After all, everyone else in Calgary did.

A Madhouse, Only With More Elegant Jackets

The Malevolent Cotton Candy Over Soyosan

Being a reprint of the reminiscences of Simba, Gentleman Adventurer

Chapter One

The Malevolent Cotton Candy Over Soyosan

"Excuse me, sir, are you Simba?"

Ah, the burden of fame! Even in the opulent surroundings of the Shilla Hotel, in the heart of Seoul, it seemed that I, Simba, had not escaped the orbit of my reputation. While others bear these obligations with ill grace, I know and respect my fans rather better. I looked up from my breakfast (a fairly adventurous combination of the local delicacy *hotteok*[19] and Special K) with a wry smile, locked eyes with the inquiring waiter, and said, "Guilty as charged, old chap."

"Very good. If you could just autograph this?" He handed me a piece of paper. Scanning it briefly, I became rather confused.

"Er, this is a bill, you know. Napkins or publicity photos—or an issue of my top-drawer periodical *Simba Adventures*—are more usual."

"I should explain, sir—Mister Harris said you could, ah, take care of his breakfast."

Suddenly the truth dawned on me—and as if the ₩ 40,000 bill (padded out, I might add, with three double scotches) wasn't enough, I was even more crestfallen when the hapless waiter pointed out the 'Mister Harris' in question. In the corner, sucking on the ice cubes of his third round and avoiding my gaze, was a pale man with a mop of unruly hair and a threadbare shoulder-padded designer jacket. I patiently sat there fuming until he glanced my way, whereupon he offered a token wave. Gripping the bill like an unexploded bomb, I marched over to this irritating acquaintance's table.

This irritating acquaintance was itinerant actor Harrison Harris. To say the fellow was not a friend would be like calling the Iron Man a bit of a jog. The last time we met, he helped release a medieval warlord as part of a festively evil plan to ruin Christmas (and you wouldn't believe how [20]). I was struck by how Faustian the whole affair was—Harris's vanity, and his myopic hope that diabolical forces might give his career a bit of a boost, led to his complicity. So despite his lack of rudimentary scruples, I gave Harris the benefit of the doubt and decided he was probably misguided. So he was lucky enough to go unpunished—although as his next film appearance was 'Second Hot Dog Vendor' in *Oscar Meyer: The True Story*, some might say karma supplanted conventional justice.

He held up his hands in supplication. "I really appreciate this, Simba. And look, here's an IOU…"

"I'm not having any of that, Harris! You can jolly well stow it!"

At this point he burst into tears and crumpled into my arms. "I'm so sorry Simba, I promise I'll pay you back! The studio cut off my expense account after last night's trip to the casino, I don't know anyone else in Seoul. Even my agent won't return my calls. You're my only hope, Simba! Please, just give me a chance!"

I looked around to see the other breakfasters staring stonily at me.

"Bravo! What a performance!" I exclaimed, understatedly clapping and rolling my eyes.

Harris looked up and wiped tears from his eyes. "And to think, *Variety* could only call me a 'journeyman actor'. But you know, Lazenby had to put up with this his whole career…"

"I'm prepared to hear you out," I sighed. It was better than another lecture about George Lazenby's misfortunes.

"Perhaps … over a quick drink?"

"Oh, my pleasure." And so, several minutes later, I sipped on a cup of Gunpowder Green tea, and Harris grumpily fiddled with the straw on his ginger ale. "It's for your own good, Harris. It's half-past ten in the morning and you're so alcohol-sodden, a misplaced match would turn you into a human Christmas pudding. Anyway, tell on—if it's especially pitiful I might even pay for your lunch."

"So after the Oscar Meyer thing work was even harder to come by," he explained. "It's the classic actor's dilemma: one day you've messed up seven takes giving Samuel L. Jackson a Smokie, the next day nothing. You ask what comes next. I pitched a TV show but no one will take it. It's a Ricky Gervais-type idea—I call it *Celebrity Self-Pity.*"

"It sounds a bit insular. Aren't there bigger issues you want to tackle?"

"I know exactly what you mean … it's kind of a dream of mine to do an exposé of the Screen Actors Guild's voting process. But I've got to be careful." He leaned closer to me. "Speaking of being careful, I may be in some trouble with—certain military forces."

Had I been sipping on tea, I would certainly have spat it out. But this was one of those moments where I didn't quite let the information sink in; I was just happy to let it rest on the topsoil of the mind. I just tapped the table lightly, and asked him to repeat himself. I didn't want to get into a tizzy; for all I knew, he might mean some Civil War Re-enactment Society from his homeland.

But he didn't. "OK, it's … an army. The New Ottoman Empire[21]. Look, there are these nuns on Mount Soyo. Real heavy nuns, let me tell you."

"That seems a bit rude to mention."

"No, no. I mean, they're into all that Zen stuff, mental exercises … so I came out here because of this rumour that they've got Provok locked up in there."

"Would it be terribly ignorant to ask who this Provok is?"

Harris shook his head in bafflement. "Abel Provok? You've really never heard of him? He's only one of the biggest criminal minds ever held in captivity. Completely unprincipled, wanted by everybody, allied with most of the major anarchist and terrorist cells still going. I think he was really big with the CapiTerrorists[22], back when they tried to retake the Northern American States."

"He sounds like *delightful* company. Why the devil do you want to get in touch with him? Are you looking for a new agent?"

"Ha, that's funny," he rejoined without mirth. "I thought I might be able to low-ball him for the life rights to his story." No doubt seeing my incredulity, he shrugged. "Hey, biopics are always good business, and these CapiTerrorists are devoted to using the anarchic potential of the dollar to undermine the government— win-win, right?"

"So what happened? Please don't tell me you met him and he's nice to his mother and loves animals."

"So after I went up to their temple—yesterday, I guess— General Mustafa is breathing down my neck. *They* want their hands on Provok too, think they can get to the nuns through me."

I nodded. "I'm starting to think whatever you're mixed up with, I might *want* plausible deniability."

At that moment the waiter came over to me. "Um, excuse me, Simba? There's a call—she told me to say that she's your aunt, she's calling from Mombassa, and she doesn't have much time, sir."

"Oh dear, Aunt Adrienne. She'll want to make sure I landed in Seoul safely, tautological though that is. Look, I'll be right back, don't go anywhere."

Bless her, Aunt Adrienne's rather an old-fashioned soul; in spite of the massive reduction in long-distance calling rates, she still thinks it's the 1970s and she's going to blow her monthly phone bill on one overseas call. Therefore, after filling me in on how cousin Chinua was finding Environmental Studies at Kenyatta University, she rung off.

I returned to my tea to find Harris gone, his place cleared. I tapped the shoulder of the obliging waiter and asked him where the old chap had gotten. I certainly wasn't expecting him to shake his head and say simply, "Sorry sir? I don't recall anyone else sitting there."

"Back me up, fellow diners!" Fat chance; they merely shook their heads and made other pantomime gestures of ignorance and befuddlement.

"Then I suppose that 40,000 won bill must have vanished with him?" I waved the bill triumphantly.

"Maybe it was your bill?" he suggested, indicating my signature as though it closed the case. Seeing my apoplexy, he quickly added, "I'm sorry I can't help you sir. I don't remember."

"OK... OK," I OK'd, as I slunk away from the restaurant and headed up to my room. I brushed my teeth pensively, pacing all the while. I was troubled by this turn of events, especially in view of Harris's earlier comments about military forces. Had he been spirited away? And what of this Provok character? With those two threads dangling before me, I felt I had to look into this.

I gargled my mouthwash as I further cogitated over this problem. It was that irritating hotel brand of mouthwash that bubbles away, leaving the hapless gargler foaming at the mouth. But this seemed fitting, for this mystery had me rabid with anxiety, and responsibility. I owed it to Harris to get to the bottom of it—and I could always go up the Tower tomorrow!

With this resolution in my mind, I changed into a more adventurous pullover—a dark red one with diagonal stripes—and a midnight blue Regency-style piped jacket. I grabbed my final two sartorial armaments—my pith helmet, and my new and rather exciting shooting stick[23]—and felt truly ready to face any danger...

I decided to take a stroll through Namsan Park to collect my thoughts and figure out a cohesive strategy. I had two clues in hand and three more in my head. The three mental ones were the names Harris checked: General Mustafa, the nuns, and Abel Provok. In my hand there was Harris's IOU and the bill from breakfast, which I couldn't have consumed on my own without a stomach pump handy. But it was more than deception—that waiter seemed genuinely confused, as though his memories had been tampered with.

Harris's IOU was conveniently written on the back of a business card with his Korean address: 331 Sogongno. I decided to start there. I was sure he'd be sitting there, having a (Conquistador-strength) Spanish coffee and a good laugh at pulling the wool over my eyes.

I brushed my teeth pensively, pacing all the while.

The apartment building was a forbidding, squat construction in the shadow of the Jongienara Building/ Namdaemun Building. I shook my head at the poor fellow's straightened circumstances: peeling paint, a doorbell that gave me an electric shock, and a handle that came off in my hand. After the nasty jolt of that doorbell, I felt like a bit of breaking and entering; although as a chunk of wood splintered away at the tap of my stick, little 'breaking' was required.

Harrison Harris's domicile was, as the saying goes, no place like home. It was a windowless and cramped space, continuing the 'peeling paint' motif of outside, its only furnishings a cracked TV and a La-Z-Boy, which, judging by the sheets draped carelessly over it, doubled as a bed. I didn't even want to see the bathroom.

And any kind of coffee was out of the question: the electrics were so shot, only someone keen on a gruesome suicide would even consider turning on the lights. Self-preservation atop my priority list, I conducted my investigation with my handy pen-torch. There wasn't much to go on: the only items that definitely belonged to Harris were a coffee-stained script entitled "Untitled ~~Michael Caine~~ Harrison Harris Project 1991" (with a handwritten note, "No thanks mate—M.C. P.S. Sorry about the coffee stains"), a couple of battered suitcases, and several drained bottles of duty-free spirits (one Balvenie, one vodka, and a peaky-coloured sake). Behind the case was a tape deck; pressing 'Play', I accompanied my investigations to the tunes of the Lost Fingers' charmingly anachronistic *Lost in the 80s*.

I heard the distant sounds of voices, getting suddenly closer. I could see from the new gap in the door that two people, a tall man and a short woman, were fiddling with the door. "Seems to be broken," the woman apologetically said.

Unsure if my presence would be taken in the intended spirit of derring-do, I slipped behind a flimsy screen and ducked into a dark, mildewed cubicle.

"There you go Mister Harris. Home sweet home, eh?" the woman (the landlady, I figured) chirped. The man nodded. I tried to get a better look at him, and was rather disturbed at what I saw.

This was certainly not Harrison Harris. Standing a few feet in front of my flimsy hiding place was a ghastly six-foot animated puppet with a waxy, lifeless approximation of his features. Its eyes were matte-black marbles. It wasn't actually *that* different from the gormless face he had over our breakfast.

The creature retched its reply in a strange, arrhythmic tempo, backed by an odd, glassy hum. "*Thank you … I do not know how I lost my key.*" Could it have been some kind of android, I thought[24]? But no; behind that cold sound there was something organic—something elemental. "*Looks like I left my tape running…*"

It walked towards the machine. It came perilously close to the alcove I was hiding in. It moved its head around, its eyes rolling around. Knowing there was only a minimally door-like piece of chipboard standing between us, I held my breath.

As if this particular tension wasn't enough, holding my breath made me aware of two other shudder-worthy facts:

I had taken refuge in the bathroom—and if the smell wasn't bad enough, I was pretty sure my jacket was brushing against the toilet (shudder!).

There was someone *else*, pressed against the corner of this tiny room, a mere fraction of an inch behind the brim of my hat. The very faintest clicking sounded behind me, so I knew then I wasn't imagining it. I suspected this other person might have been sitting on the toilet, the poor sod.

As I was contemplating all this bathroom-related anxiety, I also keenly followed the Harris *manqué*. It got closer and closer to this piece of hardboard. But then it turned around and headed out the door. "*I will … be back later … just checking on the place …*"

With the click of the door, I turned around, and saw an elegant Korean woman wearing a simple black and white nun's habit. From the dim crack of light shafting into the room, I could see her eyes widen in disbelief. She then smacked me on the shoulder.

"Hey! You shouldn't go around slapping strangers," I snapped.

"You're lucky that thing didn't find us. Great job putting the tape on," she sighed.

I shrugged airily, to cover my feelings of advanced idiocy. "I suppose I rather forgot I was mid-burglary. Forgive me, dear lady—the name's Simba." I doffed my hat. "What about you? I feel a joke about a 'bad habit' might be in order, Sister." She winced. "Fair enough—shall we step outside and discuss our mutual friend Harrison Harris?"

"Harrison Harris has to have something to do with all this. That creature we saw is proof. I must take you to our monastery."

Having said this, and before I could even offer her a hand, she jemmied the window open and slipped out. Undignified it may have been, but I quickly shinned up the wall after her—I suspected she held the answers I needed.

Chapter Two

The Malevolent Cotton Candy Over Soyosan

We sped north on the Line 1 Metro to Soyosan Station. When we got out of Seoul, I was taken aback by the breathtaking scenery and skies of Korea. Although there was an ugly black cloud hanging in the sky. Something about its glassy texture and unwavering presence made me feel queasy. It was like being watched by some judgemental, oil-drenched cotton candy.

When that comparison made me feel more stupid than unsettled, I decided to focus on conversation to distract myself. My new nun friend introduced herself as Sister Jung Kim. Considering the trip took the better part of half an hour, I was a little surprised at our conversation—or rather, the lack of it. I mean, to me, if you're with someone on a train journey and neither of you have brought a book, it seems only natural to make an effort. And one of my (admittedly few) faults is a tendency to waffle on in such situations—on this occasion I believe I was discussing how I hadn't had a really nice pie in a while. Through it all, she remained pensive and silent.

Being a sensitive soul, I sensed her brooding was out of concern for Harris. Ever mindful, I steered the conversation back to him. "Sorry, sorry! Doubtless you're completely baffled by all this jabbering about anchovies being the special ingredient in a really first-rate shepherd's pie! I'm not sure that's even true. So, how well do you know old Harrison? I must say I'm surprised he sought out your monastery; never struck me as much of a spiritual person. I'd have thought his idea of religious enlightenment would be an open bar during a firework show. Maybe I've misjudged him?"

Sister Jung stared at me as though I was wearing an Ascot tie with flared chinos. "Harrison Harris," she said slowly, "is a self-serving idiot who may have endangered all our lives."

Not sure how to tackle this particularly sanguine statement, I nodded. "Yep, well, nice as it is to know my judgement is solid, it begs the question: why the blazes were you hiding in that dreadful shack of his?"

"He was only interested in a certain criminal in our charge."

"He mentioned that—would that be Provok?" She nodded. "I've never heard of him—why are you looking after him? What's supposed to be so special about him?"

"You won't understand all the details, but he is a very dangerous presence, and our powers are all that hold him in place."

"Sorry to sound sceptical, but what does that mean? Do you keep him busy with knitting? Put on very absorbing am-dram?" She sat silently, her eyes burning with anger. I forgot I was dealing with a lady of the cloth, and my general bonhomie was taken as brusqueness, even ignorance. "Sorry, sorry—I didn't mean to offend you, I do genuinely want to know, and help."

"I'm sure you think I'm being rude—I'm just not used to talking with people on the outside." She paused. "Our collective psychic energy keeps him contained. He's an expert at psychic manipulation—as you saw from that creature he's sent out to replace your friend." I blinked. "I know it doesn't make a lot of sense. The Mother Superior will explain it better."

"Don't worry, I'll suppress my natural *esprit d'escalier* when I meet her. It comes from my upbringing—'make jokes, not war', they say where I come from."

"I don't think that's quite how it goes." She put her hand on my knee. "So, you were saying about this shepherd's pie?"

From Soyosan Train Station, we spent another half hour trekking up the rather imposing face of Soyosan, also known as Mount Soyo. I patted myself on the back—not only did the shooting stick come in very handy for helping with my footing, but my 'chukka' boots proved eminently practical. I could have hopped up that mountain if I wanted. I only slipped seven times, and Sister

Jung was kind enough to help me up. Truth be told, I was quite impressed with Jung—she bounded up the mountain several paces ahead of me. Still, this was a regular commute for her.

The temple was a new construction, about twenty metres above the Jajae-am—a legendary hermitage founded by Wonhyo, who found his enlightenment there around 645 A.D. It was easy to feel some of the transcendental ambience there—the mountain, and the nearby Tapdong Valley, seemed steeped in sublime majesty.

As for the nuns' new temple, it was an awe-inspiring sight—partly for its apparently impossible architecture (jutting ninety degrees from the mountain-side), partly because of my growing anticipation of a cup of tea that I suspected the nuns would make rather well. Jung led me through its palatial Great Hall—marble Buddhas rubbed shoulders with ornate crosses and menorahs. "Sort of an all-in-one monastery, I see," I observed.

"We take sisters from all faiths. We're trying to promote cross-denominational dialogue."

"And what do *you* believe in?" a voice boomed from the far end of the Hall. A short woman of about forty, with a somewhat sour face, strode in. She fixed me with an imposing stare. "The Mother Superior has to approve all visitors. I certainly hope you haven't been bringing in strays, Sister Jung." Her words carried a sarcastic bite.

"I know it's unorthodox, Sister Mi-Ju. But he knows Harris," Jung said. From their expressions I wondered if that was such a good thing to admit to.

I turned to Sister Mi-Ju. "My dear lady, I assure you I have the utmost respect for all your beliefs. You could call me a pantheist. It makes writing Christmas cards quite an ordeal—I *always* forget Ahura Mazda."

The three of us then had quite a staring contest, interrupted by two distinct voices—one baritone male, and one elderly female—bellowing at each other.

Mi-Ju pursed her lips. "Well, you may as well come this way."

She led Jung and me into another rococo chamber. Across from the woman I assumed was the Mother Superior—a regal, bony-faced Korean woman in her sixties—stood four military officers. Their leader stood across from the Mother Superior's desk, shouting fiercely.

"I ask you once again, Mother Superior, to release Provok to us!" he demanded. "The CapiTerrorists threaten attacks on Istanbul, Turkey—they are enemies of the New Ottoman Empire, and therefore enemies of democracy!"

"You don't understand, General Mustafa." She sounded as though she couldn't be bothered to sound convincing. "Only we can keep his powers at bay. Outside he'd be unstoppable—you wouldn't be able to handle him."

At this they both paused and looked sideways at us. I jumped from the strange unison of their movements. I felt as though I should say something, so I volunteered, "Oh, don't mind me, your chat sounded terribly interesting. Er, I'm Simba, this is Sister Jung, this is Sister Mi-Ju—oh, I expect you all probably know each other."

"Yes we do," the Mother Superior answered, looking about a foot above my head. "Sister Mi-Ju," she continued, "who is this ridiculous person and why is he here?"

"Allow me to answer that," I persisted, twirling my shooting stuck for emphasis; the effect may have been blunted when I dropped the thing, but I scrambled to get it so quickly that I doubt anyone noticed. "Again, my apologies, Mother Superior, but I'm here because a friend of mine has gone missing. I expect you and General Mustafa might have met him—Harrison Harris?"

"And considering that he turned out to be the most depraved heathen imaginable," Mi-Ju interrupted, "I must question Sister Jung's wisdom in bringing this man here."

"Now steady on!" I indignantly stammered. "I certainly wouldn't take him to my maiden aunt's garden party, but I think 'depraved heathen' is a little strong."

Jung bowed her head. "I certainly didn't intend to cause offence, Mother Superior."

"There's no need to explain," she announced. "Mi-Ju, it is good that Jung has done this. Simba, you should know that your friend's irresponsibility could be very dangerous."

"On that at least we agree," Mustafa agreed.

"But Mother Superior," Jung continued. "There was something very peculiar. In Seoul, I was observing Harris's house as you instructed, where I met Simba. We both saw a strange … replica of Harris." She pulled out her camera—a tiny digital number that must have been the source of that clicking sound—and showed the Mother Superior a snap of the creature. "Does that mean that Provok has somehow escaped?"

"How can it have anything to do with Provok?" Mustafa asked.

"Harris never got to see Provok," the Mother Superior insisted.

"What if he *had* seen Provok?" I asked.

"Well…" she cleared her throat and explained very hesitantly. "He has certain abilities—we believe they came from a lifetime of meditation, experimentation… diabolism, some might say. Anyone he meets, he can conjure a 'homunculus' duplicate—a duplicate he can then control. Only our order of sisters, after years of training in psychic defence, can safely interact with him. If he met even one outsider, he could use that person's duplicate to free himself. That was why we turned Harrison Harris away."

"I see."

"Anyway, there's nothing more to say about it. Sisters, we have to discuss what Sister Jung saw—it may be serious." The Mother Superior glided out of the room, and Mustafa's barked protests seemed to bounce off her as she left.

"Nuns, eh?" I shrugged. "I wonder if there's any chance of a cup of cocoa around here?"

"Not so fast, Simba." Mustafa held up his hand authoritatively. "As a friend of Harrison Harris, you interest us—especially considering his unsavoury interest in Provok. *You* don't know anything about all this—?"

"Good grief, no. I'm mixed up in this quite unwittingly."

Mustafa nodded to his aide-de-camp. "Swordmaster Resad, what do the databanks say about Simba here?"

The subordinate officer pulled out a computer tablet and tapped it in. I didn't like the idea of my life story being so easily accessible—not least because of the unlikelihood of getting any royalties off it. Resad reeled off the facts from his screen: "Simba.

Born Marseilles, France, date unknown. Father a tax attorney originally from Ghana, mother a baroness from Chipping Norton. Some success as a writer—although nominally based in truth, veracity of written accounts difficult to verify. Has many wealthy relations, widely travelled, frequently at the centre of bizarre circumstances. Resides in Wimblington, Cambridgeshire. Enjoys Singapore Slings. Believed to suffer from alopecia. Identifying features: retrograde fashions—notably pith helmets and smoking jackets—and rampant egomania." He looked up and shook his head in bafflement. "That's it, sir."

"That's not very good, Resad," Mustafa complained.

"Indeed it isn't!" I agreed. "Rampant egomania? You'd better watch your 'databanks' don't get charged with libel!" Adjusting my hat, I added, "As for alopecia—it's quite absurd. Can't a man like hats these days?"

Resad stepped forward, edgily tapping his scabbard. "Sir, might I suggest, in the absence of Mister Harris or Provok, we ask some questions of Simba?" I raised my hands and backed away from Mustafa's trio of underlings, who now seemed somewhat threatening. Maybe it was the gleam in their eyes, maybe their Heckler and Koch automatics pointed at me, but I suddenly felt our chat taking a turn for the less-jolly.

I've always held a distrust for the military mind; it doesn't matter whether they're New Ottoman Empire, British squaddies—even, I dare say, those Civil War Re-Enactment fellows—put someone in uniform and they seem a little less human. Between you and me, I think it might be as simple as the uncomfortable footwear. However, I got the impression that General Mustafa was a reasonable cove, and was keenly hoping to be proved right.

I raised my hands in conciliation. "Now, I quite understand you wanting a piece of ol' 'Savvy Simba', but why don't we conduct ourselves a little more civilly?"

"Stand down, officers," Mustafa commanded.

As I let out a sigh of relief so loud it could have been mistaken for a belch, a waiter entered. "Uh, excuse me for interrupting, but there are some refreshments in the rectory."

Thankfully, the promise of cocoa was fulfilled in the rectory—but it's telling that we were among people who lived in stark self-abnegation. They only had the plain digestive biscuits! It seemed downright Carthusian.

While munching on this disappointingly flavourless sustenance, I heard a faint voice calling my name. Mustafa and his underlings were arguing over protocol, as Mustafa felt Resad had been insubordinate about my arrest, and they were exchanging their opinions rather tersely. Feeling a little embarrassed to be at the centre of all this bother, I decided to trace the source of this voice. Who knew me in this remote locale? Surely an autograph hunter hadn't trekked all this way?

I walked to the door. The handle was jammed, and no amount of aggressive 'shuggling'[25] could prise it open. For some reason, the combination of the locked door and the disembodied voice was quite unnerving. I cleared my throat as casually as I could. "Uh, gentlemen? Sorry to interrupt, but I think we've been locked in by that waiter fellow. Come to think of it, why would the nunnery employ waiters? You don't think that Provok fellow…"

Then I heard a new voice behind me. "Quite right, Simba. It's me—I'm Provok, just escaping now." I turned around, surprised to see the waiter standing before me. He looked entirely unassuming—barely five feet tall, with a vacuously jolly, whey-coloured face.

I was actually going to say I thought Provok had a guy in to do his laundry and cooking; but as I wanted to seem a generally on-the-ball fellow, I decided to simply nod.

"So you're Abel Provok," I sniffed. "Can't say I've heard of you."

"Impressive—there aren't many people who'd admit to such ignorance."

"Praise indeed from a man standing chin-wagging within four feet of armed officers instead of escaping."

The waiter smiled. "Oh, you're a funny one. I've already gotten to the bottom of Soyosan and am just climbing into the nuns' coach. Put your hand out and see." As you may have guessed, gentle reader, my hand went through his shoulder; the image of the waiter dispersed into smoke. "I tell you, telepathic projection's a hell of a power. Can't wait to flex my muscles a bit more."

"I don't suppose that just means you'll be hitting the gym?"

As the smoke vanished, his voice called out, "With these powers? It'll make the CapiTerrorists' previous plans look like kindergarten! Well, bye—I'm sure you won't be stuck there too long. Mean time, try the soup!"

And then he vanished. I turned around and saw the soldiers still immersed in their argument. I ran to General Mustafa and frantically pulled at the sleeve of his uniform.

"Didn't you hear any of that? Provok—he's escaped! We've got to get out of here, General."

Mustafa yanked his sleeve back with peppery abruptness. "Simba, please! We're right in the middle of a very important point of order—Swordmaster Resad is questioning my fitness to command this expedition."

Mustafa, Resad, and the other two resumed squabbling. Only I had seen the apparition. Worse, they weren't taking me seriously and there was nothing I could do. The impotent sense of futility compared with the unhappy summer I worked at a One-Hour Martinizing store. Now, as then, the path to salvation was a solitary one—this time, though, pretending to have the mumps and skiving off to Provence wouldn't help much.

They didn't even look up as I said, "I'm off, chums." I paced the lengths of the rectory, running my fingers along the stone walls and tapping them with the shooting stick. As you might imagine, this seemed a colossal waste of time, and made me feel a prize twerp. When my tapping and banging got too loud, the soldiers shot glances of half fuming anger, half tepid pity. Between this routine, the incoherent wailing, and my general despair that something terrible was about to happen, it was quite a long eighteen minutes.

At around the seventeen-minute-forty-one second mark, I caught a glimpse of salvation. It was tucked behind the nuns' recycling—a garbage chute. A few worries about the severe drop visible through the hatch, the narrow passage, and the possibility of razor-sharp blades, paled next to the need to get out of here, and to the bottom of this whole baffling business.

I was quite pleased with the two precautions I took before embarking. First, I grabbed a length of string from a drawer and looped it round the handle of the chute: this to ease my descent. Second, I took a very deep breath as I jumped.

As a gentleman adventurer, one learns to take in stride certain perils that quiet-living individuals might blanche at: rappelling up buildings, clinging to speeding trains with leather-soled shoes, nodding politely as a female friend introduces her new boyfriend and you just know he's a total jerk. High on that list of perils must surely be an escape through a ventilation shaft[26]. While I anticipated the danger and dizziness, I hadn't quite thought of how cramped, sticky, and hot the whole thing would be. The fact that I was going down, and bits of food and garbage had stuck to the walls, only added to the experience—let's just say that I wished the nuns hadn't eaten quite so much fish and *kimchi*.

I was aided by regular circular steel supports riveted into the walls. As I felt my way down the chute, the voice followed me. Though it was as indecipherable as before, I noticed it sounded like Harrison Harris's voice. I distracted myself from the eerie wails by vigorous whistling of the 'Colonel Bogey March'.

Four 'Bogeys' later—having descended a distance of around twenty-seven metres—I heard my whistling echo in a rather larger chamber. Looking down, I saw the end of the chute ahead. It seemed to drop not onto ground level, but an extremely distant and sharp collection of stalagmites and stalactites. As I climbed to the edge, I could see more of the environs. I was climbing into a large cave, beyond which the beautiful Korean skyline was visible. I was fairly certain that I was right inside Soyosan.

"Hello?" I called.

"Simba!" The voice was now clearer—and was undeniably Harris.

"Harris—where are you?"

"I'm stuck down here—I think I can see you up the garbage disposal." Suddenly, below me, the face of Harris poked out—the lustre of his skin and the green vitality of his eyes proving him the genuine article. "How are you going to get down?"

"Not entirely sure about that." To test the depth, I dropped an apple core. It sailed through the air for a good minute before it hit the rock with a pulpy splat. "I'm thinking a jump is out of the question. How did you get down there?"

"I was drinking that crummy ginger ale, and then everything went sort-of cloudy around me, and I was in this terrible limbo. I woke up here about an hour ago. I say that, but I keep blacking out so it could be longer. I feel awful."

"Some kind of teleportation—I'd wager Provok was involved. I met an impersonator of yours, and then Provok sent an apparition to lock me in the rectory and let me know he was escaping. But how did he do all this if he hasn't met you?"

"What, Provok? No, we met. Signed a contract with him. Weird guy—good talk though. Compared with some producers—"

"You met him?" I bellowed. "The Mother Superior said it would be very dangerous ... it'd explain how he got out." I was simmering with anger—the situation was far worse than I initially thought. Provok was likely out and about, and would use his diabolical powers as liberally as a first-year Philosophy student will drop Wittgenstein into unrelated conversations.

Sensing my ire, Harris changed the subject. "Look, if you aim for these piles of garbage, you'll be fine. They're about twenty feet south of the chute—must be some strong winds coming through here."

"Look behind you Harris—we're probably a thousand metres up Soyosan[27]. In the meantime ... I need to swing towards them somehow ... ah, here's a thought!" Thankfully, I'd taken my shooting stick with me, and though it was a bloody nuisance on the way down, here was its golden moment. At the bottom of the stick was a sharp point for digging into grass. I duly wedged this point into a muddy crevice in the rock, then shuffled lower and grabbed the handle. Taking another deep breath, I hopped out.

Though I didn't quite catch the wind as I anticipated, all my vital organs were blown clear of the sharper stalactites and I made a slightly undignified head-first landing into the soft piles of garbage. As I remembered to exhale, I surveyed the damage—my ankle had caught a sharp bit of rock, but my pith helmet prevented any similar cranial injury. Even my jacket was relatively unharmed—although yet more fish clung to the elbows.

Harris rushed over and helped me up. I wasted no time in slapping his shoulder with a rather large chunk of halibut.

"Hey, don't start on me—I've had a terrible day!" he wailed. "I've never felt so weak, and I left my hip-flask at home."

I softened on him as I ruminated over what was happening. "Provok seems to be using his powers to erase your existence. Maybe it's physically taking its toll. It's probably what being in a room with Barbra Streisand feels like."

"Slow down, Simba. I know the nuns gave me that spiel about psychic powers, but this is ridiculous!" he scoffed.

"Is it? The waiter at breakfast couldn't remember you. Then there was your twin. I don't know how, but I'll bet if that creature is around long enough, your own parents wouldn't remember you!"

"After last Thanksgiving, that might be for the best," he quipped weakly, shaking his head.

"Look Harris, I dare say there's *some* rational explanation for it. Hopefully we'll live to hear it. But whether you believe it or not, you should know that this is the result of your actions. And the consequences could be catastrophic!"

I dashed to the mouth of the cave, and sure enough, I gazed on that oily, malevolent cloud from earlier crawling south. "That cloud—I'll be damned if it doesn't have some connection with Provok. But how did you get in without the nuns' knowledge?"

"But they did know," Harris said. "Yeah, Sister Mi-Ju, I think her name was—she set the whole thing up. There was something about her, she seemed familiar."

"The plot thickens," I mused. "I think Sister Mi-Ju was operating independently. I wonder why? And how we can stop it?"

"We?" Harris asked weakly.

"I hope you're not trying to weasel out of this, considering it's partially *your* fault!" I thundered.

"Of course not!" Harris replied, brimming with disingenuous bonhomie. "I just meant … uh, *oui*! Sign me up, *Monsieur*!"

"As we don't have time for an acting critique, I'll just pretend that was sincerely meant. Our first problem is how the devil to escape? Is there anything around here?" I surveyed the cave area, but saw nothing of use. My ball of string would barely have gotten us to the nearest ledge of the mountain, let alone the rest of the way down.

"Looks pretty hopeless," Harris shrugged. "Just a lot of garbage—literally."

"I know. I think someone should tell the chef these nuns don't like all this fish," I smiled.

"Oh, that's not part of the garbage. They leave it there deliberately. You'll see what happens."

Several moments later, I witnessed an awesome sight that satisfied my curiosity. From the depths of the mountain, an almighty roar echoed. It was accompanied by at least thirty birds, each about nine feet across with a wingspan of about thirty. They plunged around us, vigorously attacking the fish and the other garbage, and then swooped out of the mountain into the distance leaving little debris behind. A couple of the more adventurous members pecked at my jacket sleeves, which was slightly terrifying.

"Sweet fancy Moses!" I exclaimed. "These birds are enormous—next to them an albatross would look like a common pigeon!"

"Scared the hell out of me the first time I saw it." We both stared into the horizon, following their long and effortless flight.

A crazed thought suddenly struck me. "Wait—the first time? You mean they fly through here regularly?"

Harris nodded. "Must be quite a few of them. They go every hour or so." He double-took. "You can't be thinking…"

I beamed. In retrospect I might have been suffering from low blood sugar, but at the time it felt essential to keep positive. "Think about it, Harris. If we stand near the cave mouth, and jump as they fly by, we stand a definite chance of catching one. It is a bit of a long shot…"

"A long shot? Are you kidding? I'd *rather* be in a room with Barbra Streisand than do this! At least I'd have a stuntman."

"If only Provok's plan was as simple as a re-release of *The Prince of Tides*. What did he say during this ill-fated meeting of yours?"

"Oh, I don't know—usual psycho stuff, the powers of creation and destruction … something about focussing mental energy to create harmony. He kept going on about a single perfect moment, how could he harness this moment, that kind of stuff. I wasn't nearly drunk enough to follow the conversation—he sounded like a New Age Hannibal Lecter. And would you believe he hadn't seen any of my movies?"

"Well, he has *some* taste. But that sounds significant. This temple is an impossible piece of architecture, the nuns' mental energies secured Provok, you unbalanced it … damn, it's not a lot to go on!"

My agitation was joined by hunger. It was nearly three in the afternoon, and my breakfast had been on the light side. We munched on a couple of mints, but that only made it worse—there's a time of day when only a sandwich will do. We then passed the time (about fifty minutes in all) with a round of my favourite game, 'Spot the Famous Quote'. It proved quite absorbing—especially after the third time Harris used lines from his movies as a quote, when we argued quite strongly over whether *The Finger-Lickin' Good Film*, or anything directed by Alan Smithee[28], could be considered famous. He countered that such a rule was a bit rich coming from me—citing such 'ludicrous' (his word) *Simba Adventures* titles as 'Crouched Behind Some Convenient Coral', '1500 Words About Spider Zombies', and 'Don't Hurt the Head on That Heir!' I failed to see his point. It all got very childish.

Then, from the dark edge of the cave, the sound of massive wings flapping echoed, and my heart was filled with hope and excitement. A grandiose flock of about twenty of the birds soared over our heads, stopping to pick over the remaining fish. Best of all, they came just as Harris was looking up *Pies: Feet of Fate*'s North American grosses on a ridiculous computer contraption called a 'BlueBerry'[29].

"Never mind that!" I cried. "Now's our chance!"

Chapter Three

The Malevolent Cotton Candy Over Soyosan

We both scrambled to the edge. The birds were violently careening down the side of the mountain. I plummeted over the edge, my stomach tingling nervously. The birds had flown so far down that we were in mid-air for a good twenty-three seconds before the birds were in range. I grabbed the thick chestnut feathers on the bird's back, slightly afraid of how it would react. Luckily it seemed unfazed. I fell forward, and at that moment it pulled up and flew towards the sky.

There was an odd moment when it turned its head and quizzically looked down its beak at me. As we locked eyes, I wasn't sure what to say. "Much obliged, my dear … bird!" I exclaimed. Though they seemed entirely incapable of speech, I thought I saw a fractional nod from the proud beast. I then looked up to see how Harris was coping. He seemed a bit peaky, but successfully clung to his bird, lying against it with his arms tightly gripped around its neck.

"Why did I let you talk me into this?" he screamed. "I was happier in the cave!"

"Oh go on!" I called back. "Look around you! We've got a front-row seat on a majestic miracle!" I sucked a lungful of brisk air and basked in the gorgeous sunlight, and the mountains and plains of Korea's skyline. I seized the oasis of calm, and tried to convince myself that maybe the extraordinary trials that lay ahead wouldn't be quite so bad.

Onward the flock soared; our speed, I estimated, fifty kilometres an hour. We luxuriated in our surreal airborne spectacle for a good hour before a new worry popped up. I decided to consult Harris—even though he hadn't exactly been sage counsel up to now.

"Harris—it occurs to me that we have no control over these birds, so I'm not entirely sure how we're going to land… any thoughts?"

Harris shot me a bitter look and glanced over the side at the 200-metre drop.

"Part of me wouldn't mind seeing you go the obvious way."

"That comment was beneath you, Harris. And let's not forget—"

"I know, I know, 'my part in all this'. I have no idea—hang on, here's something." He slapped the side of the bird. It squawked angrily and did an agitated barrel roll. I know I shouldn't have, but he was just so hapless that I had to laugh a bit.

"We're not riding into Tombstone to see off the Clantons, you know!"

"*I KNOW THAT! WHAT THE HELL DO YOU EXPECT ME TO DO, YOU ST*PID J*RK? I'M COMPLETELY TERRIFIED RIGHT NOW AND I WANT TO GO HOME!*" he yelled, his face scarlet with fury. Though I didn't feel he needed to call me such offensive names[30], I was probably being a little irritating, and decided to work on it myself and get back to him.

And the brighter side of things seemed to be clearing off with indecent haste. About seventy feet ahead of us, the spectral cloud hove into view. As we drew closer, I could feel a cold blast emanating from it, and a hum of malevolent energy. With it a chill ran down my spine, and into my heart.

As our flight path came nearer to Seoul, across a small river from a large ornate temple, I noticed an upturned coach, with plumes of smoke billowing from it, and two figures racing across the bridge.

"I know that place," Harris said. "That's Gyeongbokgung; 'Palace of Shining Happiness'. Built in 1395. I went there on my second day; nice place."

Onward the flock soared; our speed, I estimated, fifty kilometres an hour.

"Well, I'm fairly certain that's the nuns' coach on fire there. And you'll be thrilled to know that I have a plan to get us to ground level."

By chance a rather large fish had remained in my breast pocket (there was *quite* a lot in that cave). My sadness over the silk handkerchief in the same pocket was outweighed by my joy at its utility. I dangled the uncooked mackerel in front of the bird's vast beak. Its head darted from side to side, so before it snapped my hand off, I dropped the fish. As I predicted, the bird glided down after it; Harris's bird and a few others on either side followed suit. I looked back at him and gave a thumbs-up, but Harris still looked sceptical.

As the birds touched to the ground, we their grateful passengers, dismounted. Aside from my aching ankle, I greatly enjoyed the experience, and I gave the birds an appreciative tap on the head. They chirped their approval. It was rather heart-warming.

We passed several awestruck locals—it isn't every day that colossal birds drop in for some fish. Sister Jung stood beside the overturned coach, shaking her head.

"Simba!" she exclaimed. "How did you get here?"

"We, er, took the scenic route," I murmured. "Oh, I suppose you know Harrison Harris." Jung gave him the thinnest of smiles, so I glided over the subject and indicated the burning coach. "Provok, I presume?"

She nodded grimly. "He just appeared in the coach, and before we could do anything he flipped us over and took off with Sister Mi-Ju. She helped him escape. I just can't understand why she'd turn on us like that."

"I can answer that," Harris interrupted. His BlueBerry screen displayed a behind the scenes photo from *Pies: Feet of Fate*. Standing beside a fibreglass prop foot was unmistakeably Sister Mi-Ju. "I thought she looked familiar—she's American, real name's Nellie Jamieson. She had sympathies with the CapiTerrorists even then. I didn't blame her—she had a tough time, living with the shame of parents in the Tea Party."

"But it's worse than CapiTerrorists," Jung insisted. "Provok's completely unbalanced. They headed in there."

"So, why the Gyeongbokgung?" Harris asked, scratching his head. "It's a beautiful building—admission was a little steep, but not dangerous."

Jung "You probably didn't get to see the strange abyss discovered in an underground cavern about three hundred years ago. So many of our historic sites were destroyed by the various Japanese invasions, and the theory is that the invasions released so much deep trauma that the physical environment was affected. Mister Harris, your Salem, Massachusetts is believed to have something similar."

"Leading to…?" I pointed up to the black energy cloud. Jung nodded. "Some kind of dimensional instability—exactly the physical means for Provok to infinitely enhance his abilities. How's that for a scientific explanation, eh?"

Harris stared at me as like a faulty tongue dispenser. "Are you serious?"

I raised an eyebrow at Sister Jung, who kept a diplomatic silence. "Tsk! Didn't realise I had to impress Niels Bohr over here. My dear Sister Jung, where's the Mother Superior?"

"Back at the temple. I sent for her, but she'll take at least an hour to get here."

"In that case, I think we'll have to go in on our own."

We were about to head in when a tank trundled out from the other side of the Yeongjegyo Bridge, flanked by jeeps and marching soldiers clad in military-flagged tan regalia. Swordmaster Resad popped out of the tank, and his voice blared from a loudspeaker. "Simba… surrender now."

"I'd love to," I called back, "but I'm a bit busy preventing an inter-dimensional disaster."

"We know you've kidnapped General Mustafa—"

"General Mustafa? What happened to him?"

Resad explained: "After you crawled down the garbage disposal and we'd formally instituted procedures to relieve the General of command, there was this strange smoke, and then he disappeared. As you had left shortly beforehand, we put two and two together."

"Not me, Provok! He teleported Harris to the cave inside the mountain, he must have done the same thing with General Mustafa—no doubt as a hostage. I'd wager my Christmas bonus[31] it has something with the enhanced powers he's getting from that cloud."

Jung nodded sagely. There was a pregnant pause as Resad considered this. Indeed, the pause practically went into labour before he announced, "I still think we should take you back for questioning before we investigate this."

"There's no time for that! Don't you care about your superior officer?"

"You'd think that. But I've got his job now. I went five years without a promotion! And I know you think, 'Ooh, Swordmaster sounds like a good rank', well do you know what my per annum salary is?"

Alas, I never found out; Sister Jung tapped my arm and indicated we should press on. Doom might fall before Resad finished complaining. We each grabbed one of Harris's arms and went across the bridge.

We approached the Geunjeongmun gate, collectively ignoring the progressive drops in temperature. Through the gate we trudged, and from there to the Great Hall. The Gyeongbokgung is normally an ornate construction, with red pillars, boldly primary-coloured architectural buttresses and sharp angles visible up to the roof. But these normally vibrant colours were muted by the haze of thick smoke through the building. The daylight from outside didn't penetrate the windows. The atmosphere too felt cloying and constrained.

"Reminds me of a Friday night down at the Institute of Learning Disabled Llamas delivery office," I coughed. "Those delivery chaps can knock back a cigar or two. If only the danger was as simple as second-hand tobacco-smoke."

Reinforcing my point, Jung pointed to some shadowy shapes shuffling to the throne at the end of the Great Hall. The familiar glassy hum filled the air. Next to the Harrison Harris *manqué* stood one with the likeness of Sister Mi-Ju, identically matte-eyed and humming weirdly. The creatures were an appropriately gruesome-looking couple in these surroundings. Keeping a safe distance, we followed them as they walked past the throne to a sliding wall panel.

Things only got darker as we descended a spiralling staircase, and as we neared the bottom the sickly hum had grown so loud that my head practically throbbed along with it. What light there was glowed dimly, like the dying embers of a campfire. In that murky orange, I caught a glimpse of Provok, wind from the massive abyss swirling around him. Mi-Ju stood at his side, and over in one corner sat General Mustafa, his face paralysed in abject terror. As we got closer it was imperative to blend into the background so we could assess the situation.

Sadly, Harris stumbled at an uneven step (and it was so dark at this point, I could hardly blame him) and fell face first down the staircase. I promptly tripped over him, and Jung followed suit over me. The three of us reached the eerie subterranean altar in an undignified heap.

Provok stepped towards us and offered a hand up. "Er, much obliged," I muttered. "Sorry to blunder in like this."

He slapped me on the back. "Think nothing of it! And I'm glad you could make it, Mister Harris. What do you think of your double?" Harris could only shrug, completely overwhelmed. "And Sister Jung, care to join your cohort?"

"Absolutely not!" she spat, refusing to take his hand as she stood. She crossed over to Mi-Ju, and grabbed her by the shoulders. I was taken aback by the bald-faced rage she showed. "How could you—desecrate what we believe in?"

"What *you* believe in," Mi-Ju rejoined bitterly. "I've seen my country brought to its knees, and Abel Provok is the only one who can restore it to its rightful place. That's worth any cost."

"Exactly!" Provok nodded jerkily as he sprang up to the void. "But with this … do you know what I can do?"

"Well, you certainly don't need any help generating hot air[32]."

"That's a brave card for *you* to play, Simba. But time as we know it doesn't exist on the other side of this. I understand you have some experience with extra-dimensional realms outside time."

"I've dabbled a bit," I admitted. "Although you could say that of anyone who's been to Coventry."

Provok turned back to the void. Its howl grew ever more hypnotic. I started to lose perspective of the room around us as Provok continued talking. "You'll thank me—so will everyone in the world. The reaction of the two dimensional states will cancel cause and effect, and create a moment of stasis. A nirvana, a single, eternal high all around the world."

"Controlled by you, though!" Jung observed.

"Yes, me and my creatures." He motioned towards the assembled Harrises and Mi-Jus. "Not you, though. Nor General Mustafa here—he proved too strong-willed to duplicate."

"I refuse to surrender my faith in the tenets of the New Ottoman Empire," he stoically declared. My admiration for General Mustafa grew.

"OK, fair enough—you'll be sucked into nothing-ness with that blasphemy on your lips," he said flatly. "How about you, Simba? You could be an equal partner."

"Mmm—what kind of holiday time are you offering?" Don't be horrified, dear reader; my mulling was only an ingenious ruse while I weighed the scale of the crisis and if there was anything around I could possibly use to turn the tables. Sadly, I could barely comprehend the nature of this schism; not only did Provok hold the winning hand, he also had shares in the casino and was married to the croupier's sister.

"Eternity—like I said. Come on, not much time left!" The volume of his voice see-sawed with his varying emphases.

Before I could answer—with a droll *bon mot* along the lines of "Get stuffed, you fanatical git!"—Harris scrambled up the dais.

"What about me?" he asked. Jung and I both shook our heads, possibly with a little slack-jawed disgust thrown in. "Come on, guys. I come from Hollywood. They call back-stabbing good business there. So what can you offer me?"

"Selling out your comrades, purely in it for the big dollar— that is so CapiTerrorist! You're in!" Provok beamed.

I just had to interrupt this smarmy rogues' conference. "Call me a thicko, but what possible value will money be in a world where cause and effect are laid waste?"

Harris looked sideways at his new confederates. Jung added, "How can there be a bottom line when there's no bottom?"

"Exactly—well said, Sister Jung!"

"Irrelevant!" screamed Provok.

This seemed to relax Harris. "So, what now … buddies?"

"Now? We throw you in and see what happens." Provok threw Harris towards his simulacrum, now wreathed in plumes of viscous black smoke. As Harris stumbled closer to the widening schism, they froze into a disturbing tableau, the one writhing in agony while the other stood in triumph.

I think we all realised that this wasn't going to be much fun.

Provok sucked air through his teeth. "Don't take this personally, Harrison. I really appreciated your help."

As pandemonium erupted around us, Jung pulled me towards her. For a strange second I thought she was leaning in for a kiss.

"Er, it's been nice knowing you, Sister Jung …"

"Wait, Simba! I think I might be able to help Harris. If I can use the Mother Superior's training…" She closed her eyes and slowed her breathing. Then, her voice no louder than a whisper, she recited a mantra, repeatedly intoning the same Tibetan words over the howling wind and billowing smoke.

She frantically gestured that I should move towards the schism. I was completely consumed by the almighty pressure in the air, but in the absence of any logical alternatives I obeyed. I crept closer, my vision dominated by the two Harrises; they seemed to be melding into one being.

"What's the point?" the genuine Harris shrugged. "May as well go along …"

"*Exactly … will anyone really miss you? Who … really needs an actor anyway?*" The creature's voice carried a horrifically bitter ring, and Harris nodded, his entire body hanging limply in mid-air.

"Think, Harrison!" I urged. "Whatever you've done counts for *something*. Think of *Celebrity Self-Pity*!" As my eyes locked with his, I made my last point count. "What would George Lazenby do?"

"Damn it, Simba, you're right," he croaked. "*This* never happened to the other feller." With a pained wrench of his wrist, he propelled his simulacrum backwards. It rose and slowly shook its head. It then looked over at the Sister Mi-Ju duplicate, then they both nodded. As the simulacra stepped between Provok and the ever-widening schism, the criminal's beaming mask seemed to slip.

"OK, guys, bring it in, sure," he nodded.

"*Sister Jung's psychic defence has freed … us of your control.*"

"Jolly good—I wholeheartedly support your independence move!" I called out. "And you should know this rotter was planning to abuse your powers to control others. How do you feel about that?"

"That's not true!" Provok yelped. "I was trying to make things better!"

"*The resources of our dimension … are not yours to abuse and cannot solve your problems …*"

"But I can give you money—millions of dollars from the CapiTerrorists' funds! All yours if you help us!" he shrieked hysterically. They looked across at each other and turned back to him.

"*This is … meaningless to us*[33] *… your ambition is … selfish and narrow-minded … we must now … restore the balance.*" They started to merge together, into a gigantic claw of black smoke. The claw gripped Provok and pulled him screaming into the chasm. As it wrenched shut, their strangulated tones echoed through the cavern. "*We will leave the others … in your hands … Simba and Sister Jung … we regret the … inconvenience.*"

Chapter Four

The Malevolent Cotton Candy Over Soyosan

General Mustafa, Sister Jung, and I exited the Gyeongbokgung—now restored to its natural lustre. To be on the safe side, we held Harris and Sister Mi-Ju between us. Across the bridge from the palace, the Mother Superior and her fellow nuns stood, their faces stonily impassive. Resad's tank stood to the side, its pilot pinning new rank insignia to the swordmaster's lapel.

I stopped in front of them and a few other curious bystanders. After this strange ordeal, I had some difficulty summing up my emotions.

After some thought, I announced, "Rest easy, everyone. Sister Jung and I, Simba, have just saved you from … a Seoul-destroying experience."

The sound of a hundred-strong crowd groaning echoed through the Gyeongbokgung courtyard.

"Oh, come on!" I cried. "OK, it was a bit corny, but after all I've been through…"

The Mother Superior turned to her acolyte. "Well done, Sister Jung. Your mental fortitude is inspiring to us all." At Jung's insistence, the nuns thanked me as well, but I brushed it off. It was partly my natural humility, but also because I was incoherent with hunger[34]. I left them to clean things up and caught the nearest cab to the Shilla Hotel. My future sanity depended on three immediate courses of action: a bath of at least an hour and forty-five minutes; a reviving plate of smoked-salmon sandwiches with a quart of ginger beer and a large glass of Malamado Malbec port; and a much-needed change into smoking jacket and cotton moleskin trousers.

So, it wasn't until late that night that I felt ready to meet Sister Jung and Harrison Harris to discuss the many fascinating issues of our adventure. We met at Sanchon, and over a bottle of *gukhwaju*[35] and some rather delicious *kimchi*, I felt equilibrium had been truly restored—well, aside from a bit too much seaweed with my flat-cake.

Jung caught me up on the day's fall-out. All trace of the schism had vanished, and the Mother Superior had confined Mi-Ju to the monastery until her psychic powers dissipated. And the New Ottoman Empire was going to give me the Order of the Sultan (which, as well as sounding pretty cool, also gave me preferred parking anywhere in Constantinople!). This chat naturally segued to Harrison Harris's fate.

"You're welcome, by the way," Harris mugged. "Oh come on. That whole 'going over to Provok's side'—it bought you guys the time you needed to turn the tables." I pursed me lips, and felt inclined to treat his words as utter poppycock, and possibly throw him under the nearest bus. Seeing my scepticism, he seized my wrist desperately. "Please ... consider that when you make your decision, eh, old buddy?"

"What do you mean?"

Jung revealed, "Simba, General Mustafa has let you ... decide Harris's fate."

"Really? *That* should be fun. I wonder how I'll decide?" Maybe it was a bit mean, but considering the inconceivable damage Harris nearly unleashed, I felt the very least I could do was keep him squirming until the appetizers arrived.

"All right, Harris—I'll give you the benefit of the doubt. May as well cling to some shred of optimism about human nature." Harris leapt up and down and flung his arms around me in joy.

"Thank you, thank you Simba! I won't forget this—how about a trip to LA when my new movie comes out?"

"New movie?"

"Oh yeah. My agent called—he's got me a cameo role in this movie called *Scientology A Go-Go!*. According to his website the director's been called 'a talent reminiscent of Uwe Boll and Brett

Ratner, with the working practices of latter-day Fritz Lang.' It can't fail, right?"

I smiled and raised my glass. "Karma—you've done it again."

Endnotes

Simba and the Charles Dickens Caper

-Chapter One

[1] The Institute of Learning-disabled Llamas was founded in 1962 by Norris Humperdinck with a mandate to investigate and cure common educational afflictions among llamas. Since then it has expanded to include a library covering many arcane topics, numerous monuments, a champagne vineyard, and a diamond-encrusted radio telescope. While learning disabilities among llamas are impossible to detect by lay-folk, Humperdinck and his successors have insisted that they do exist, and at a cost of £56 million annually, it's really "a bargain".

[2] Simon Callow: Superlative actor, who, among his other achievements, is regarded as the foremost Dickens interpreter of his generation. His Dickens appearances include the one-man show *The Mystery of Charles Dickens* (2000) and the classic *Doctor Who* episode *The Unquiet Dead* (2005). Course, he was also in *Ace Ventura: When Nature Calls* (1996), but we're not prepared to hold that against him, seeing as he's such a splendid chap.

[3] "Peerless turn of phrase," I chortled.

-Chapter Two

[4] Simba was of course referring to popular Welsh actor Ioan Gruffud, who starred in a 1999 Masterpiece Theatre film of *Great Expectations*. He notes, "That'll teach Carroll for saying I never bother to look things up."

[5] Simba would like to categorically state that said aunt has confessed to her addiction to barbecue sauce, and is trying to wean herself off it.

-Chapter Three

[6] This adventure is chronicled in *"Simba Adventures 138: Passport to Perfidy!"* Sadly it is now out of print, and only available in the collectors' edition. And don't worry, Simba got off scot-free, the blighter.

-Chapter Four

[7] In the interests of the more sensitive readers, Simba elected to omit this very offensive word. However, the curious might like to know that the first sentence of every paragraph on the following two pages spells it out. Go on, it'll be fun, and who knows—you might be surprised!

[8] Recounted in *Simba Adventures 223: "Terror on Toast!"* Also out of print, but nobody really minds as it wasn't a very good story.

[9] Institute of Learning-disabled Llamas. Do keep up!

[10] It doesn't.

-Chapter Five

[11] So you see, that's why they weren't returning Jasper's calls when Chad and Doris were asking him tough questions in Chapter the Third. With service like that, I doubt Jasper would particularly recommend them.

[12] Albert Finney didn't play Thomas Hardy, so far as can be ascertained, but Simba just always thought that's what Thomas Hardy would have looked like.

The Empty-Headed Architect

[13] Cthulhu (either "Khlul-hoo" or "Ka-THOO-loo") was a demonic octopoid entity created by H.P. Lovecraft in the 1928 story "The Call of Cthulhu". It has a devoted following, particularly amongst university students, but is purely a figment of Lovecraft's imagination ... OR IS IT?! *(Yes it is—Ed.)*

[14] For reasons of libel, the name has necessarily been obscured. But go on, see if you can guess who it is!

[15] After the Great Elitist Exodus of 2047, the farthest right fringe of Conservatives, to demonstrate their strong opposition to intellectualism, actively refused to teach their children how to speak. In their opinion, this created a freer, more emotional form of democratic expression.

[16] Blimey, only scientists could produce a monster that was so damned condescending.

[17] And OK, many were quick to add, "Not that we endorse your policies, mind you." It still struck a nauseating note.

[18] Called in to deal with strange faculty activities, the Direw University Peer Review Committee are some tough monkeys. *(Don't send them thesis proposals on Ghostbusters, take it from me—Ed.)*.

The Malevolent Cotton Candy Over Soyosan

-Chapter One

[19] A Korean pastry, usually with a sweet filling of honey, brown sugar, chopped peanuts and cinnamon. This endnote was written late due to the editor's demand that at least four actually be informative. See if you can spot the other three.

[20] See "Children of the Coal" in the *Simba Adventures Christmas Bumper Number.* As for Harris's part... he was impersonating Santa Claus. What's that? Don't say you're one of those old-fashioned squares who doesn't believe in the big red guy! If so, you'll presumably be infuriated to learn that it wasn't even the first time Simba dropped in on the North Pole's First Family. But those improbable escapades must remain unpublished—at least until a lucrative book tour beckons.

[21] The New Ottoman Empire was formed to counter the international clout of allied Pacific Rim nations in the late 21st century. On his appointment, new Sultan Aleem Abdulla (a 21-year old M.B.A. from McGill), promised "a dynamic brand synergy, with greater emphasis on today's marketplace than on fezzes and conquest." The enterprise has met with widespread acclaim. Despite alarmist fears of religious and racial persecution (and disappointed fez-fanciers), in practice the Empire has lived up to, and expanded on, its predecessor's diversity.

Their only embargo is against the cast and crew of *Sex and the City II*, who are expressly forbidden from entering Dubai due to that film's disgraceful line "Abu Dabhi Doo!"

[22] CapiTerrorists™: A group of self-styled 'American patriots' who believed in a system of commerce-based anarchy. They engineered 'corporate terrorism' on and off (mostly off) between 2062 and 2097 with the aim of re-forming the United States of America along pre-Civil War lines. They were frequently hamstrung by the fact that their plans were never as unscrupulous as the banks they sought to supplant. Their leader, known only as 'C.O.O.', is believed to be hiding somewhere near the ruins of MIT. Despite rumours of corporate training camps, he has only been sighted in instructional videos of blood-curdling boredom. In line with the CapiTerrorists' creed, they are massively overpriced, at $1,175.98 US; ironically, every major government is too cheap to pay, so only subscribers know what their demands actually are.

[23] A shooting stick is a wooden walking stick with a folding leather 'seat'. They're ideal for walking and gadding about in fields, and are a more portable embodiment of the 'director's chair dream': you can truly have a seat with you anywhere you want to go.

[24] Completeness demands a note that Simba has plenty of experience with androids. Why, in this very collection, 'Simba and the Charles Dickens Caper' attests to that.

-Chapter Two

[25] Simba notes: "The term 'shuggling' was coined by my work mate Norm to describe the particularly agitated rattling that one performs on a stubborn doorknob, often pointlessly and accompanied by angry kicking of the attached door".

[26] This is admittedly not a ventilation shaft. But as the modern ventilation shaft usually has the same circumference as shoeboxes (compared with the halcyon 1960s, when they seemed purposely configured for Sean Connery to shinny up and down), the reader must grant that it's as near as dammit.

[27] Soyosan's actual elevation is 587 metres (Simba notes waspishly, "I was somewhat preoccupied at the time!"). But hey, what else are endnotes for, right?

[28] The interested reader may be surprised to see the many credits of this versatile, yet almost unknown, Hollywood director (highlights include *The Birds II: Land's End* (1994) and *Mighty Ducks The Movie: The First Face-Off* (1997)). His films are uniformly contentious and controversial—exactly the sort of thing someone might get embarrassed about and remove his/her name from. But Alan Smithee proudly graces the credits of some lamentably atrocious films. Some claim he's a pseudonym, but he certainly seems as real as Michael Bay and Jon Favreau.

[29] Simba's ignorance of developments in computer technology should be no surprise to long-time readers of his chronicles. Any thought that Harris's device might be a blatant copyright dodge is entirely correct: the 'BlueBerry' was developed using stolen technology by a Swiss Mom 'n' Pop concern whose name has vanished, along with their tax returns. It offers a depressing footnote in history: its chief innovation—edible (fruit-flavoured) circuitry—proved handy when it was launched during the notorious Geneva Famine. Therefore, an un-eaten example like Harris's is worth as much as its more famous competitor, which you'd be advised to trade it in for: edible circuitry has sod-all processing power.

-Chapter Three

[30] In fact, he added a few more offensive epithets, which Simba did not record due to poor sound quality and his oft-stated concern over their suitability for "members of the fair sex".

[31] The previous year, due to lack of funds at the Institute of Learning-disabled Llamas, this bonus had been reduced to a fiver and a box of Lindt chocolates—just a plain bar, not even the special Christmassy ones. So, impressive though it may sound, Simba was hardly putting much on the line here.

[32] Some critics have suggested that 'hot air' gags are completely obvious and unnecessary, but Simba insists that he couldn't avoid it—like how when any vaguely villainous character says someone's "tied up at the moment", you know they've performed the offending bondage themselves.

[33] As this confirmed his point about how worthless their money would be, Simba contemplated dropping a "Told you so" here. But quite enough was going on as it was.

-Chapter Four

[34] Simba stubbornly refuses to admit that his "Seoul-destroying" quip might have been a product of this hypoglycaemia.

[35] A wine made with chrysanthemums—see, don't tell us these endnotes aren't educational! (*That only makes three, unless you're counting the one about the shooting stick—Ed.*)